When It Rains It Pours

When It Rains It Pours

By

Rosetta Mandisa

Sula Too Publishing

ISBN-13: 978-1-7339542-1-1   Paperback

Library of Congress Control Number: 2019946574

Printed and bound
In the United States of America
January 1, 2021
10 9 8 7 6 5 4 3 2

Published by
Sula Too Publishing
Tampa, Florida
www.sulatoo.com/publishing

Dedication

For my first born,
Saleem Tyreak

Contents

Acknowledgements

This book is a book of progression. I have read and re-read the pages in this book off and on for the past twenty years or so. As I struggled to understand childhood trauma and the toll it was taking on my life at such a young age, I spoke openly with my high school counselor. She gave me two pieces of advice that I still use today, read and write. She encouraged me to read as a distraction so that I wasn't too overwhelmed by what was happening to me and to write in a journal as often as I could to get out the words that swam back and forth through the quiet places of my mind. I believe those two things saved my life during time when I felt completely lost. It wasn't until I got much older that I learned to use my voice. Speaking about my trauma has also helped tremendously.

As a young girl, I lost myself in books. When my thoughts, anger and rage became too much to bear, I wrote in my journals, journals that I still have to this very day. After my son was born in 1993, I wanted to be the best mom I could be and knew that there were things from my past that still plagued me. So, I decided to write "my story" hoping it would help to alleviate some of my pain. I bought a spiral notebook and began writing. Over the years "my story" has moved from the notebook to a floppy disk and finally to a thumb drive.

Along my life's journey, there were so many people who impacted my life in positive ways. I would like to thank Ms. Ersula Odom-McLemore of Sula Too LLC for believing in me and my story. She brought to life what I've been carrying around in my heart, head and computer for the past twenty years. I cannot thank her enough.

I would like to thank my very good friend, Jewel Rainey. She was the first friendly face I met at my new job just after I moved to Florida many years ago. She continues to check in with me and always has a positive word for me. Sheila Denise, my spiritual big sister, thank you so much for studying the bible with me and helping me to rebuild my relationship with God. Thank you for not giving up on me the many, many, many times I wanted to throw in the towel. To my 3SB Crew, Janice and Caksher, you ladies make sure I laugh and laugh often. Thank you for your encouraging words and for always answering the phone when I call.

To the women at Soroptimist International of Tampa, who I proudly get share volunteer services with, all of you are truly amazing. Thank you for your guidance, your prayers, your hugs and smiling faces. I cannot tell you how much you have blessed my life.

Lissahn DeVance, lady we have seen some rough times together. However, we have also seen some truly amazing times as well. Thank you for never letting me quit on my dreams and for setting a positive example. I pray that Enraptured Events will continue to be all that you've dreamed it could. Miss Cydney

Charese, you inspire me, and I love you so very much.

Thank you to Mrs. Maude E. Crumpler for putting up with my childhood shenanigans, paying tuition so that I could graduate from high school, making sure I had food to eat and clean clothes on my back. Thank you for loving me unconditionally, listening to all of my frustrations and family drama, never judging but always having a word of encouragement. Thank you for treating me as if I was one of your very own, for making sure my son had a great head start in life and for always reminding me not to get large. I love you with everything in me.

Consuela Stewart-Crawford, you will forever be the very best thing that could have happened to me. You became a part of me when we were nine years old and I could never repay you for all that you have given to me. My life would not be the same without you. I was able to overcome because of you and for that, I will owe you for life. As always, we shall take it to the grave!

To my littlest and wisest advisor, Nokomis Taylor, thank you for being a seven-year-old phenom. I always enjoy our talks and your wonderful advice. Whenever I feel a bit discouraged, I remember your voice saying, "Don't give up, Auntie Ro! No matter what, you just gotta keep trying." I love you, Pies!

My grandmother, Mrs. Lillie Mae Dunn turned 88 years old this year. She is an amazing woman who taught me what it means to be strong and independent. Thank you, Gran, for being the best example for me to model my life after. Thank you for always answering my calls and for letting me hide out at your house.

Even though they are no longer with me, I would like to

thank my parents, Mose and Minnie, for loving me as best they could and for trying even when they weren't sure how; my brother, Zachary Dunbar, for simply being the best big brother a girl could ask for and my brother-in-law, Freeman Jones!, for being the best inside joke partner a girl could ever have. I miss you all every day.

To my brother, Frederick, a.k.a Freddie P., thank you for always having my back.

To the members of the Brinson/Moore family, thank you for allowing me to be a part of your clan. You have always shown me love and it is truly appreciated. I have enjoyed getting to know all of you.

I have the most amazing nieces and nephews in the world! Thank you, Silas, Deshawn, Andrew, Lonntay, LaToya, LaTasha, Domonique, Tia, Tiona and Anthony! Thank you all for being such positive, beautiful, hard-working, well-rounded young people. I am proud and grateful to be a part of your lives.

My sister, Angela Jones, you are the best. You have always been my protector. Thank you for always having my back, for helping me to stay focused on my goals and for reminding me that I am valuable.

To my love and life partner, Wayne Moore. I am still amazed at our journey thus far. Thirteen years and counting. Thank you for never trying to clip my wings and giving me room to fly. No matter what crazy idea I get in my head, you are my biggest cheerleader. I will never get enough of hearing you say, "what are you laughing at." I tell you; you missed your calling as a comedian. Thank you for always trusting me with the best part of you; Derrius, Jaylen, Breanna, Jaden, James, Madison and Zion.

To my son Saleem, Kiddo, you are still the reason mommy works so hard to be her absolute best. I am so very thankful and grateful God saw fit to bless me with such a handsome, outstanding young man. Keep pushing toward your dreams and never give up, Landon and Teigan are counting on you. I hope my work has blazed a trail for you to follow so that you, too, can reach your dreams. You are my heart and the air I breathe.

With love and a humble, grateful heart,

Rosetta

Living life is never an easy task. If you ever sit down to really think about it, life can sometimes be down right horrible. That is one thing I learned early on in my quest for greatness. Becoming an adul takes understanding and a great amount of skill. The understanding comes when you learn from your mistakes and believe me, you wil make a lot of those. Skill starts at birth. You have to know the key to survival in order to stay alive, like, crying when you are hungry and crying really hard when you want a clean bottom.

Life is, in a way, drawn out for you. It starts the moment you enter preschool. School is supposed to be the time when you learn al the basic life skills. You know, things like respect, being polite, and treating others the way you want to be treated. Through your years of institutional learning, you start to dream about what you'd like to become when you grow up. A firefighter, a lawyer, a police officer, a teacher or an advertising executive are all professions parents would be proud to have their children a member of. After elementary schoo. where you kissed your first boy, middle school where you failed P.E and high school where you got all confused about the birds and the bees, you are then supposed to go off to college. College is where you are supposed to get the education that will help to make you famous someday and also, between pledging, making lifelong friendships, and growing into a productive citizen; find the mate you plan to spend the rest of your life with. Your parents get to come to your graduation and a few months later they get to throw you the biggest wedding your side of the neighborhood ever would see. You get the dream job and after two or three years you begin to produce those offspring your in-laws are always bugging you about. And you live happily ever after, right?   Wrong! Whoever wrote that line of crap must not have ever thought about what happens when life throws you a curve ball. I'll tell you one thing if you are not well prepared a curve ball, fast or slow, can throw you right off track.

Your parents are your teachers of lifelong skills. But then again, they are not perfect so sometimes you have to rely on your own understanding and the life skills you've developed. When you're thrown in tight spots, you can't always assume that your parents or anyone else can squeeze you out. If I close my eyes and think hard enough, I'm sure I can remember the first time life threw me a curve ball and it was a serious one. It had to be…the Fall of 1987.

Chapter One

Nobody Likes Change

"You're getting a what?" I wanted to scream. I know I must have heard her wrong.

"Baby, I said your father and I are getting a divorce." Yep, that's exactly what I thought she said.

I can't believe it! My parents! Divorced?! Just the thought of it makes my stomach turn. All I can think of at this moment are all the friends I have whose parents are divorced. They spend summers and weekends with their fathers and the rest of the time with their mothers or vice versa. I don't want to live like that. She must be out of her natural mind. Ha! That's it! My mother has lost her mind.

"Girl, are you listening to me?" my mother asked interrupting my thoughts.

"Huh! What?" was about all I could manage to get out.

"I asked if you were listening to me."

"Yeah, Mom I'm listening to you."

Mom kept rambling on and on about how things had been going bad between her and my father for quite some time. I could barely hear or comprehend everything she was saying. I think I just heard bits and pieces and then somehow put it together.

"Aeysha, I need you to be strong and there is no need to be afraid." Mom was interrupting again.

"May I go now?" I don't think I even waited for a response. I just knew I had to get out of there.

I ended up downstairs in my room. I had just enough strength to lie across my bed and think of all the strange stuff that's been going on with my parents lately. Just about a three months ago my family moved in with my mom's friend Teresa. Mom said it was so that she and Dad could save money to buy a house. Well, so much for a new house and definitely on the chopping block was having my own room.

I wondered how my brother and sister were going take the news. I can almost picture their reactions in my head. My brother has always thought that my parents had the perfect marriage. With him being the oldest, he's been around them longer and my poor sister is the spoiled middle child. I don't think she will know what to do without my dad's pockets to dig in on a regular basis.

They are the lucky ones; they don't have to live here or be around to hear this madness right now. My brother, Tyrone and his fiancé, Bobbie live not too far from Teresa's house. My sister on the other hand is still in Alabama at my grandmother's house. She was planning to finish the school term and then move back home once my parents found a house. So, my mom's news this afternoon is will most definitely throw a monkey wrench in her plans. I am back to my original thought; my mother has lost her mind.

Looking out of the window, it seems to be turning out to be a nice day. I wish I was out there in the sunlight, but I can't think of one place I'd rather be right now. My friend Shawna, who lives at the end of the block, is at her dad's for the weekend. My best friend, Joann lives all the way on the other side of the bridge and that is a bus ride I'm definitely not up for today.

I must have stared out that window long enough to bore myself to sleep because the next thing I remember is being startled awake by Joan and Sheila stumbling into the room.

"Aeysha, what are you doing?" Sheila said while bouncing on my bed.

"I was sleeping. Now could you please get off my bed?"

She jumped right off my bed and turned on the television set. Ugh!

"Sheila, could you turn that down." I said.

"Shay, why don't you get up? You are not going to lie in that bed all day." Joan said.

As if it was any of her business! She gets on my nerves. I really wish my parents had come up with a better idea than to move into this place. This house may look big on the outside, but with all the people living inside it is very small. Talk about crowded. Not only do my parents and I live here but also Teresa's mom, Mary and Teresa's sister Joan. Teresa's two kids Mimi and John Jr. and Joan's daughter Sheila also live here. Let me not forget John's girlfriend Janice who lives here from time to time when they are not in some heated battle about who knows what. Amazing…I didn't forget anyone.

Since it looks like I won't be getting any sleep. I guess I could sneak into the kitchen and call Joann. When I got to the top of the stairs I could see that mom and Teresa were sitting in the living room, drinking coffee and talking to some man I had never seen before. Oh, well. I am not in the mood to see or talk to my mom so I continued on my quest to make my secret phone call.

"Hi, Jo." I said when she picked up.

"Hey, girl. What happened to you today? I called earlier but Teresa or somebody said that you were asleep."

"Yeah, I had some stuff to sleep off. Mind if I stay over next weekend?"

"Oh, please! Since when you have to ask to stay over?" Jo laughed. "Hey, you don't sound like yourself. Are you okay?"

"No! You know how it is over here. I'll tell you about it when I get over there next weekend. Let me go, you know I can't get caught on this phone."

"Okay. I'll see you Friday"

"Yep, right after school. Bye."

After Jo hung up, I held the telephone receiver a little while longer. I wanted to call her back just to talk. I needed something to keep my mind from racing. I'd lost any interest in going anywhere this weekend. I just couldn't function. My life was not going at all how I thought it would. Still in shock and thinking parents simply cannot get divorced.

Friday couldn't come fast enough for me. As the week dragged on, I noticed that my mom started acting strange. She walked around the house as if nothing happened, like she had not just sent my world spinning out of control. The weirdest thing was that she had started staying out all night. That was very unusual for my mom. She had always been home when I went to bed. This week I think she might have been here two nights. Mom actually seemed happy despite recent events.

My dad was going to be home soon. Maybe she had changed her mind about this whole divorce thing. My parents have been married for fifteen years. I cannot remember a time when they were not happy. Even though my father worked as an independent contractor and was on travel assignments most of the year, they seemed to make it work. Well, I'm only a thirteen-year old kid, what do I know?

The bus ride to Joann's house is about the longest ever but on this Friday, I didn't mind it at all. I had to get away from that house even if it was only for two days. Right after school, I ran across the street to Teresa's house, grabbed the overnight bag I'd packed the night before and headed for the bus stop.

I should've taken the commuter train, after all it is faster. I just hate being on that thing when we have to go under water to get into San Francisco. So… the bus it was. When we pulled up to the Oakland toll plaza, traffic was backed up as usual. Off the bridge to the right you could see all of the beautiful high-rises in downtown San Francisco.

One more bus and I will be at Jo's house. Being at her house was the best. I could always be myself when I was there. Mrs. Commons, Jo's mother, is the sweetest person that ever walked this earth. Not long after I started staying over, Mrs. Commons told me that it was okay to call her Mom or Mommy. I guess calling her Mrs. Commons in her own house every five minutes was just nerve wrecking. I thought that was a very nice gesture and I knew that she wanted me to feel comfortable when I stayed over.

"What took you so long?" Jo was hanging out of her

mother's bedroom window when I turned the corner.

"You are crazy!" I yelled.

No sooner than I got in the house we were laughing and talking so loud our voices echoed off the walls.

"No, Jo!" I said between screams of laughter. "You are lying!"

"I am not!" Jo managed to say.

She was telling me a story about this guy she'd met at school. It was so funny even her mother had to laugh.

"After all that I hope he was cute." I said.

"Of course, you know I don't mess with ducks."

I laughed so hard at her that my stomach ached. That's how it always is when she starts talking.

Joann is the world's greatest best friend. We met each other about five years ago at a church both our parents attend. A few weeks after I met her, we begged our parents to let us have a sleepover. I stayed the very next weekend at her house and now it's just natural for me to stay nearly every weekend.

Did I mention that I love being at Jo's house? I don't have to pretend to be someone I'm not or keep quiet when I need to talk to an adult. Mommy let's me tell her anything. I can always tell her when things are bothering me or when my mother and I are having a difference of opinion. Mommy and Jo give the best advice and they never judge me.

By late Saturday night Jo and I were still going at it. Jo told me the latest gossip at her school, and I spilled all of the beans I had stored up for the week about the crazy girls and pitiful boys at my school. We were laughing and talking so loud Mommy had to yell back to Jo's room to tell us to turn off the television and go to bed.

"You girls aren't going to want to get up for church in the morning" she said. Mommy has to tell us that every weekend that I stayed over. It never fails.

Jo got up to turn off the lights and the television.

"So, are you going to tell me what's going on with you? And don't even try to lie. You know that I know you better than you know yourself." Jo whispered to me in the dark.

She's definitely right about that.

I told her the whole sorted story about how my mom was planning to divorce my dad. Somehow, I was able to remember nearly word for word what my mother had said to me last weekend. Even though I knew Jo wouldn't mind, I refused to cry. I was not going to let this divorce ruin my life. I was still hoping my mom had changed her mind about the whole crazy idea.

"Shay, I'm so sorry to hear that." Jo said.

"Don't worry about it, Jo. I'm not going to."

"I just can't imagine your parents divorced. Your mom always looks happy."

Little did we know then the source of her happiness.

Sunday seemed to have come and gone in a flash. Mommy never missed church on Sundays. No matter how many services were held on that day, we were there early and attended them all. Since Jo and I didn't have to sing in the choir or serve on our usher committee this Sunday, we'd wandered just outside the church doors to see which of our church friends were going to show up for morning services. Just before Sunday school started, we saw a few familiar faces and talked with our friends in the vestibule until an adult came along to point the way to our classes.

When the last service was over, Mom met me in the parking lot so that I could transfer my bags from Mommy's car to ours. This was the part of the weekend Jo and I dreaded. We'd hug until one of our parents pried us apart and forced us into our respective cars. The way we carried on, a person would have thought we were never going to see each other again,

"Call me as soon as you get home." Jo shouted as her mom drove away.

"See ya!" I yelled back.

A few weeks after that trip to Joann's house, I noticed some very strange things happening with my mother. I simply could not put my finger on it and I had a sinking feeling whatever it was, I was not going to like it. It seemed like I hardly ever see my mother any more. When I get up in the morning to go to school she's gone and she still isn't at home by the time I go to bed at night.

I even had to start taking the bus back to Oakland after church on Sundays because she hadn't attended service or come to pick me up. There was definitely something weird going on because mom has always been good about going to church. I've noticed that she comes by Teresa's house maybe twice a week now. She'll stay an hour or two talking to Teresa and poof! just like that she's gone again.

Monday afternoon when I got home from school there she was. She acted as if a whole week hadn't gone by since she'd last seen her daughter.

"Hi, baby girl." Mom said with a big smile.

"Hi, Ma." I shot back.

"Well?" She said.

"Well, what?" I asked.

"Don't I get a kiss? You haven't seen me in a while."

Like that's my fault. I kissed her on the cheek just to make her happy. However, I was more concerned about the disappearing acts she'd been pulling.

"Where have you been hiding?" I asked.

"I've been working double shifts. So, instead of crossing that bridge every night, I stay at a friend's house in San Francisco."

"Oh. That's nice." I said turning to Teresa. "Where's Mimi?"

"She hasn't gotten home from work yet. What do you need?" Teresa replied.

"I just need her to sign this permission slip so that I can take a computer class after school on Tuesdays and Thursdays."

"You haven't asked me anything about staying after school." Mom said. Sounding like she might be a little upset.

"Well, Mother if you were home to ask maybe I would have." Oops! That didn't come out right.

"Excuse me. What the hell did you just say to me?" Mom was on her feet now. I'm dead!

I didn't answer her. I don't know what to say. All I know is that right at this moment I am suddenly very mad at her. For the last month and a half Mimi has been signing papers I bring home because she has not been here on days that I needed things signed. Now here she comes acting all offended because she hasn't been on her job as a parent. Don't look now Mom, but your daughter's not stupid and she is growing up a lot faster than she'd planned to.

"Bring that paper to me!" She yelled bringing me back from my thoughts. I was on the run now, might as well finish the race.

"Why? You haven't been here to sign the others. Mimi will sign this one when she gets home just like she always does!" I was screaming at her.

"Shay, I really don't care what the hell you do but, I suggest you get your smart behind out of my face before I hurt you."

She took one step toward me and I turned and ran downstairs to my room. How dare she try to come in here and tell me what to do? Granted she is my mother but she has got some nerve. Never once did she ask me if I wanted to stay here with Teresa and crew while she works 'double shifts'. I don't like being treated as if I am too young and too stupid to have an opinion.

At the very least she could have told me ahead of time that she wasn't going to be at home much so that I could have been prepared. Instead she pulls a disappearing act and expects me to be okay about it. NOT!

I had stayed in my room and didn't even go up when Teresa called down to tell me dinner was ready. Mimi brought a plate of food to me when she came down to my room to sign my permission slip.

"Hey, Miss Aeysha. Mom told me that you need me to sign something."

I handed Mimi the piece of paper and she signed it with no questions asked. Mimi was usually the only one that called me by my given first name. Most everybody else called me Shay. I could always count on Mimi to say my full name as if she was a little more proper than her ghetto, Oakland upbringing.

"Aeysha, my mom also told me what happened today when your mother was here." Mimi said.

"You mean to tell me she's gone again? I guess I shouldn't be surprised." I said.

"Aeysha, try not to be so hard on her. She is going through a rough time right now." Mimi's last words as she walked out of my room.

Mimi maybe twenty-one years old but she'll never understand what I'm going through. Her parents got divorced right after she was born. They never lived together for years like my parents. I know that my dad works away from home a lot but, when he is home we are a regular family.

But I guess, at thirteen I still have a lot of growing up to do if I am ever going to understand adults. I had to take a bath and be in the bed before Joan and Sheila came in. I definitely didn't want to talk to or see anyone else right about now.

Chapter 2

Thanksgiving

Thanksgiving break was finally here. My teachers were really starting to work me. It seemed like every week there was a paper due. Joann and I had been spending quite a few of our weekends at the library. My mom has planned for us to spend the day with Teresa and her family at Teresa's ex-husband's house. Oh, what fun!

On Thanksgiving Day, my mom called to tell me that she wasn't going to be able to pick me up for the trip to Big John's house in Hayward. She didn't even bother to tell me why. She just said that I'd see her there.

Teresa put me in the car with Janice since she was riding by herself. I felt a lot like an orphan. My mom hasn't done anything with me in a while. Maybe, just maybe I will get a minute or two of her time while we are out at Big John's. She has to be missing spending time with me too.

The ride to Hayward was about thirty minutes. Janice talked the whole time about stuff that she and Little John, L.J. for short, were planning to do before the baby got here. I must have been completely wrapped up in my life because I didn't even know she was pregnant.

When we pulled into the driveway L.J. and his friend Robert were waiting outside. I think Robert is just the most handsome, young man I've every laid eyes on. I hope he didn't bring that girl he's been dating. He always dates these tall and very thin women. A little too thin I think. I grabbed my bag and headed for the house.

I think I might need to see an optometrist because I know my eyes must be failing me. My mother is sitting here, in front of everybody hugging a short, bald, gray headed man! And if my eyes are working properly, they're holding hands! Aaaahhhh! I can not believe that this is the first thing I get to see when I come into the house.

"Hey, Shay." Mom said.

"What are you doing?" I had to ask.

"Oh, honey, this is my friend Paul."

"Hi, Shay. I am glad to finally meet you. Your mother talks of you all the time." Paul said. It speaks!

Who is he and why is he talking to me? I didn't want to cause a scene so I said hello and walked away. I could tell that everyone was watching. I guess they were waiting to see how I would take meeting my mom's new 'friend'.

Big John told me which room to throw my bag in and I did as I was told. The house was big and beautiful. Nothing like I'd ever seen before. On the way to my sleeping quarters I passed two bedrooms downstairs and three upstairs. Now this is a house. I sat down on the bed and turned on the television. There is nothing like a little Soul Beat to pass the time. I just love watching music videos. They seem to make a song that much better because you now get a picture to go with the music.

"Hey, little lady."

I looked up and Robert was standing in the doorway. He has the nicest smile and a great set of white teeth to go along with it. I'm sure L.J. told him that I have the biggest crush on him. But Robert never let me know it. He always treats me like I'm his best friend.

"What are you doing up here all alone?" He asked.

"Watching Soul Beat of course." I smiled. "Are you following me?"

"Of course." He smiled back. "Come with me."

"Where are we going?"

"Just get up."

Everyone was in the family room at the back of the house, so Robert and I walked out of the front door and down the street. He was cool to hang out with. We only talked a little when he came to Theresa's because he and L.J. were usually in a hurry to get somewhere. So, he was gone almost as soon as he got in the door. As we walked, he told me some crazy stories about times he and L.J. go out to clubs in the city. It sounds like they have fun but, I don't think clubs will ever be my thing. They seem to be overcrowded with people and loud.

Robert was at Teresa's house just about every weekend picking up L.J. so they could hang out. And from the way he was talking now, they got into more than enough trouble.

"We should turn around." Robert said.

"Yeah, look how far we've walked. They might serve up the turkey without us." I said.

On the way back, Robert held my hand. I thought I was

going to faint. He was always doing little things like that. When he comes in the house he hugs me real tight, if no one else is around that is, he kisses me on the forehead and sometimes he'll even play in my hair. I should be used to it by now but he always catches me off guard. We both know that there is a big age difference between us and I know that he goes out with women his own age. We have that unspoken respect for each other.

Mental note: I must call Joann when I get back. By the time we arrived back at the house everyone was ready to eat.

"Where have you two been?" L.J. asked. "You're holding up the feast."

I had to laugh because no matter what was going on, L.J. was always ready to eat. Big John blessed the food and then it was time to dig in. The grown-ups took their plates into the dining room. I knew I would have felt out of place being the only kid there so I stayed in the kitchen.

I did, however, sit in the chair closest to the dining room so that I could hear what was going on. I heard Paul ask my mother if I was okay about him being there. She said she was sure I was and that she'd speak to me later. The conversation in the dining room got boring after awhile so I focused my mind on my food. It was truly good. Big John knew how to cook. He had all of the Thanksgiving staples; turkey, stuffing, cranberry sauce, ham, collard greens, yams, string beans and an assortment of deserts.

No sooner did I get up to turn on the small television in the kitchen did Robert come in and turn it off.

"What are you doing?" I asked. "I was watching that."

"Yeah, right, like you know anything about football." Robert said.

"I do!"

"Want some company?" He asked.

"Why not, you turned off the game."

"I just wanted you to know that I had a great time with you today." Robert whispered.

"It was fun. Thanks for inviting me." I said hoping I didn't sound too juvenile.

Just then Mimi called him back to the dining room. Five minutes later he came back and was standing over me.

"Are you finished?" He asked.

"Yep! I think I am stuffed."

"You want to go to the store with me?" He asked. "They need more ice and beer."

I walked in to tell my mom that I was riding with Robert to the store. She was still wrapped up with the old guy and just waved her hand as I turned to leave. I can not believe she has barely said two words to me since I've been here. I mean really. She was so tied up with "It" that she didn't even notice that I had left earlier with Robert.

Robert drove a very nice 1988 black Toyota Celica. Even better, it had a drop top. Robert let the top down for me. My hair was all over the place. The one time I needed one, I didn't have a ponytail holder in my pocket.

Our conversation on the way to the store was basically small talk. Robert asked me about school. I asked him about work. But on the way home Robert's voice seemed to turn a little serious on me.

"Why are you so quiet now?" He asked.

"I'm just enjoying this wind in my hair." We both laughed.

"Well, tell me something about you." He said.

"There is not much to tell. You know how old I am, where I go to school and what I do when I'm at home since you're there so much."

"Are you complaining?" He smiled.

"Of course not. Why don't you tell me something about you?" I asked.

"You can ask me anything you like." He said. "But nothing too personal though."

I decided now was as good time as any to find out exactly how old he was. My gosh, when he said twenty I thought I was going to pass out. I knew he was older than me but not that much older. I do know one thing; I have got a lot to tell Jo. She'll never believe he's that old.

Back at the house, mom was still hanging on to what's his face. I can not believe how she is acting. She's a married woman. I hope she's not divorcing my dad to be with that old thing. I can't wait for my dad to get home. He'll straighten her out and it will serve her right.

"What are you staring at?" Robert asked.

"Nothing!" I shot back.

"Hey, don't bite my head off. I was just asking a question." He said.

"I'm sorry. I just can't understand what my mother is trying to prove by bringing that man here."

"Who, Paul?" He asked. "That's Big John's brother."

"What! You can not be serious. Now that you mention it, I think I may have seen him at Teresa's house talking to her a few months back."

"Yep, well now you know. So be a doll and take this glass to your mom."

How could he be so calm about this? My mind was racing. Big John's brother! No wonder no one else was as surprised as I was when I first saw them together today. As I walked out of the den, mom told me I should go to bed. She said I didn't need to be up with grown folks.

I tried explaining to her that it was a holiday and that I didn't have school tomorrow, but she was not hearing it. I think she just didn't want me around because I reminded her that she was married with kids. She couldn't have a good time with me lurking around.

Robert whispered that he'd come keep me company as soon as he could get away.   That made me smile. I guess he figured since we were the only two there without a significant other we might as well keep each other company.

I was upstairs watching television for what seemed like hours before Robert finally showed up. He sat on the floor and watched the last forty five minutes of the movie Grease with me. That is my favorite movie of all time. There was nothing on in the room but the television. Robert didn't say anything and neither did I. Personally, I liked the quiet. But it also made me nervous.

"So what's going on down there?" I asked when the movie went off.

"Not much.   They're downstairs loud talking and bull joshing." He answered. "It looks like your mom is having a ball."

"Imagine that. I don't know what her problem is, but I hope she gets over it real soon." I said.

When I looked up to see why Robert hadn't responded, he was looking directly in my face. The strangest thing happened next. He kissed me. He pressed his lips softly on mine. I was seriously nervous. What if I wasn't doing it right? I wouldn't want him to laugh at me. But then again, why should I care? He was the one who kissed me first.

"You are really cute." Robert said after he finally let go of my face.

"Thanks, I guess." I didn't know what else to say.

"Do you mind if I kiss you?" He asked.

"It's a little late now, don't you think?" I said. "Besides, don't you have a girlfriend?"

"Not now. I haven't had a serious girlfriend in six months. You haven't seen me with anyone, right? I'd always brought a girl to Teresa's house when I go out with L.J. and Janice."

"You lie. That doesn't mean anything." I had to laugh because he knows that I hear all the stories about his and L.J.'s club experiences. The room got quiet again.

"So, do you mind?" He asked.

"What?" I knew exactly what he was asking. I was trying to put off answering that question for as long as possible. I wasn't all that sure that I wanted him to kiss me again. I liked him and all, but I still couldn't say for certain that I was ready to play this game.

My question was answered for me when Robert leaned over to kiss me again. Oddly enough, I didn't pull away. The longer we kissed the more comfortable I began to feel with him. I was certain he wasn't going to try anything else especially with my mom right downstairs.

Staring in his eyes, I told Robert that he should get back downstairs before someone noticed that he'd been gone for a long period of time. He simply hugged me then kissed my forehead before saying that he would be back later. At this point I was certain that he would return. The question was what's going to happen when he does come back? I've got to call Joann.

Before Robert could get the door closed behind him, I was picking up the phone extension beside the bed. This was one call I knew I could make without getting into any trouble. All of the adults were consumed with their grown folks' conversation in the den. My girl, Jo answered on the first ring.

"Jo, it's me." I said in a low tone.

"Hey! Where have you been? I called you today." She said.

"I am in Hayward with Teresa and my mom. The day was going kind of bad until I started hanging out with Robert."

"Robert? Isn't he L.J.'s friend that you said was really cute?"

"Yes, he is the one." I said. "You will never guess the fun I have been having with him today."

"Okay so don't keep me in suspense. Spill it!" She said.

I told her all about the walk we took, our ride to the store, and about him holding my hand. When I knew I had her all supped up, I told her about 'The Kiss'. Joann laughed so hard. She even told Mommy what I had said. She tells Mommy everything, which is a good thing because she lets us know what to look out for when we are dealing with boys. Or in my case now, should I say man?

I had to get off the phone with them. They were making me laugh and the last thing I wanted was to get caught. I told Jo that

I would see her at church Sunday and hung up. Robert did come back later, but by then I had fallen asleep. He kissed me on the forehead and said goodnight. Before I could get my eyes open all the way he had vanished out the door.

Friday morning came rolling in with bright sunlight. I got up and tried to find an available bathroom. With only three bathrooms and twelve people, that was kind of hard to do. Janice came by and said that the bathroom downstairs was empty. Walking through the living room I could see that mom and Paul were still wrapped up in each other.

"How'd you sleep?" I heard him say, but I didn't turn around.

"Shay, Paul is talking to you." Mom said to me.

"Fine!" I snapped back in their direction.

"Girl, I think you better get yourself together and drop that tone in your voice." Mom said to me, but I just ignored them both.

I had no intentions on behaving when it came to Paul. So my mother could just get that sick idea out of her head. There was no way I was going to let this stranger into my world. I was happy with the way things were. No one told her to change that. Anyway, I haven't seen Robert yet and I hope he hasn't left. I, at least, wanted to say good bye.

My attempts to get an empty bathroom had failed. I got to the bathroom door downstairs in time to hear water running. I knocked to ask whoever was in there how long they would be. To my surprise, who else but Robert opened the door. He was wearing a towel and a few drops of water.

"I'm sorry. I didn't know you were in here." I said. "Will

you be long?”

"No, I just need to finish shaving. Get in here." He said pulling me into the bathroom before I could protest.

"What are you doing?" I whispered.

He laughed. "I'm not going to attack you or anything."

"Very funny, what if someone walks in here?" I said. My gosh, he is even better looking shirtless!

"I locked the door and don't worry no one is going to look for you. They will probably think that you're still upstairs somewhere."

"How'd you sleep?" He asked.

"Fine and you?"

"I only slept an hour or two. I came back last night."

"I know."

Robert finished shaving while I used the other side of the double sink to wash my face and brush me teeth. He must work out often because he had a very nice body and a six pack to die for. When Robert started washing the shaving cream from his face, I grabbed the towel he'd laid on the back of the sink. I didn't know what I was going to do with it, but then he looked down at me, smiled, and started drying his face.

By the time I'd finished he'd had his arms around my tiny waist. I put my hands on his arms as he pulled me closer to him. Robert bent down and kissed me softly on the lips. I think I was beginning to like this kissing stuff, but I know that I am not ready to do anything more.

"Can I show you something?" He asked once he unglued his lips from mine.

"I'm afraid to answer that one." I said still staring into his face.

"It's not like that." He said. "Have you ever been French kissed?"

"What?"

"I'll show you."

And that he did. Robert parted my lips with his. At this point I was so nervous that I closed my eyes. I felt his tongue lightly touch mine. I wasn't at all scared. For some odd reason I just trusted Robert. Had I thought he'd do something to harm me I definitely wouldn't have been locked in a bathroom with him. I pulled back when I heard someone talking outside the door.

"I'm sorry." Robert whispered. "Are you okay?"

"Don't be." I whispered back. "So that's what a French kiss is?" Wow!

"Yep!" Robert laughed. "We'd better get out of here."

I silently agreed with a nod. We were not sure if there was anyone outside the door so he stood behind the door as I went out first. I checked the hallway and didn't see anyone coming. I knocked on the bathroom door to let Robert know that the coast was clear.

We all started leaving Big John's house at about 2:30 p.m. I just wanted to get back to Oaktown and hop a bus to Joann's. Mom was going back to San Francisco with Paul but couldn't give me a ride because they were meeting his friends at a restaurant. I had made up my mind right then that the next time I got her alone for more than five minutes that I was going to let her have it. I mean really have it. She just jumped in the car with Paul, waved good bye, and off they went.

When Janice and I got back to the house, I ran downstairs, started taking dirty clothes out of my bag and putting clean ones in. As I walked into the kitchen, I heard voices coming from the front door. One of them I knew for certain was Robert's. Sure enough he came walking in the door behind Janice and L.J. Robert smiled at me and all I could do was smile back trying not to look obvious.

"Teresa, I'm leaving now." I yelled over all the noise in the kitchen.

"Okay baby girl. Be careful and call me to let me know you've made it." Teresa answered back.

"Where is she going?" I heard Robert ask Teresa when I got to the front door.

"To San Francisco. She spends most of her weekends over there with a friend of hers." Teresa answered.

"If it's okay with you I'll take her. I have to go on that side anyway." I heard Robert say.

"Ask her. I don't care." Teresa said and turned back to finish her conversation with Janice.

I was trying to hold back the smile that wanted to cover my face. I could not believe he did that. I knew he was completely serious when he walked over to the door and said come on. We said our good byes and walked out.

"Are you crazy? I asked him.

"Why would you say that? Just because I offered to take you to San Fran?" He asked back.

"Yes! Like you really have to go to all the way over there." I said jokingly.

"I do." He laughed.

"Okay. Whatever you say."

The drive to S.F. was great. We talked about everything and nothing at the same time. He told me he'd had nice time with me at Big John's. At this point I was wishing the drive to the city was just a little longer. We pulled in front of Jo's house and just like clockwork she was in the window. Robert parked, got out and came around to open my door. He kissed me softly on the lips, said our good byes and then he was gone. Jo was at the door before I could ring the bell.

"Oh my, gosh, who was that?" Jo screamed through the gate.

"Could you let me in please?" I said.

"Not until you tell who that was."

"That, girlfriend, was Robert." I screamed. "Now will you let me in?"

"Get in here. You have so much to tell me and we only have two days."

Chapter 3

And The Secret Is Out

The sound of the phone ringing pulled me away from my morning routine.

"Hello." I said.

"What's up, Sis?" The voice on the other end of the phone said.

"Hey!" I said realizing it was my sister Melissa.

"What are you doing?" She asked.

"Not much, Sis." I said. "Just getting ready for school."

"Hey, everybody's asking about you. They want to know when you are coming back." She said.

"I'm not sure and you don't sound like you're ready to come home."

"I'm not." She said.

"Are you and Aaron still together?"

"Of course." Melissa said and I could tell she was smiling.

"How's grandma?" I asked.

"She's fine and she sends her love."

"Well, tell her that I love her and I miss her."

"So where's Momma?" She asked.

Oh no! I knew that was coming. I wasn't sure, but I didn't

think mom had told Melissa what's been going on and I sure wasn't going to make it my business to tell her now. I know Melissa will be heartbroken when she found out so mom needed to take that devastation on her own shoulders. So for now, I'll just have to do what mom asked me to do if any one called and she wasn't here…LIE.

"She and Teresa already left for work." I answered.

"Well, tell her to call me back."

"Ok, I will pass on the message when I see her."

"Thanks, Sis. Have a good day at school and I will talk to you later."

"Ok! Love you!

After I hung up I felt a little sad. I missed my big sister and I couldn't wait to see her again. Hopefully, I'd get my chance soon.

It was early Monday morning and the house was already empty. Sheila and I were usually the last to leave. Since we went to the same school I got stuck with the task of seeing her to and from school on most days. I really didn't feel like babysitting this morning. I knew my mom hadn't come home last night and I hated lying to Melissa. I wish Melissa was here with me so I wouldn't have to go through all this drama alone.

"Aeysha!" I heard Sheila yelling from downstairs.

"What?" I yelled back. "I hope you're dressed for school."

"I'm almost finished, but I can't find my other shoe." She said.

"Sheila, we have to be out of here in thirty minutes and I still have to do my hair and yours. Find another pair of shoes and get upstairs."

Sheila is a nice girl, but some days I feel more like her mother than her babysitter. I have to get her up in the morning for school, make sure she has breakfast, and comb her hair. It doesn't stop there because when school is over, I have to get her home and help her with her homework. God forbid Joan has to work late. Then I have to make sure she does her homework, eats dinner, has a bath and is in bed on time.

To be eight years old, Sheila is a lot of work. Joan does thank me but won't pay me a dime. She and Teresa say that I am young and need to learn some responsibility. Easy for them to say, I might not be so upset about it if they had only asked me instead of just expecting me to do it. Personally, I think it's just a way for me earn my keep.

I could see Shawna standing by the gate at school when I stepped out of the house. Living this close to school wasn't all that bad. I didn't have to take a bus and even if I woke up a few minutes late, it didn't mean I would have to be late for school. The one thing I don't like about school is the uniform. I don't mind private school, but these plaid skirts are the ugliest things I've ever seen.

School is usually a breeze for me, but this particular Monday was really a bad day. I thought this day would never end. It started early this morning when David, a boy in my class, put a bunch of staples in my jacket while it hung on the back of my chair. When I told my teacher, Mrs. Mosley she said she'd have a talk with him but that he was just trying to get my attention because he liked me. I don't care whom he likes, I just wanted him to leave me alone.

Mrs. Mosley moved David to the back of the class for the

rest of the day. It didn't help because he kept passing notes to me. At lunch, Shawna and Denise were playing in line. Denise slipped on something and when Shawna tried to catch her, their lunch spilled all over my socks and shoes. I was so mad that I didn't talk to either of them for the rest of the day.

At the end of the day I waited at the corner for Sheila to come from her class and we walked home. It was finally over. I could go home and wash away all traces of this day.

Well the traces will have to stay a little while longer. When I walked in the front door, I was truly surprised to see my dad sitting in the living room talking to my mom.

"Hi Daddy." I said almost happy to see him.

"Hey, baby girl. Come here and give Daddy a hug."

I walked over and gave my dad a hug for two very good reasons; one, it looked like he needed it and two, because I needed it. I could tell by the look on his face that he was sad. I wanted to feel sorry for him, but I was too angry with my mom to feel anything but anger at that moment.

"Look, baby, your mother and I have something we'd like to talk to you about." He said looking down at my hand.

Before I could think about it, I said, "Daddy, I already know and I don't want to hear another word about it. It's not like mom would change her mind if I didn't want it to happen. I can't believe you're going to let her do this!"

"Honey…" Daddy started.

"No, Daddy. Mom is being selfish and she only thinking of herself and I don't think there is a thing we need to discuss."

"Wait a minute, Shay. What do you mean you already know?" Daddy's face went from sadness to confusion. Oops!

Maybe I'd said too much.

"I told her about a month ago." I heard my mom say.

"Why would you do something like that?" Dad asked mom. He turned from me back to my mom. Now he was very angry and the look on my mom's face was my cue to leave the room.

My parents rarely argued in front of me. I could still hear them even from downstairs in my room. I know that my mom must be mad at me, but I really don't care. She would have wanted me to stand there in my dad's face and pretend as if I didn't know what was going on. I couldn't do that. Daddy was sitting there trying to muster up courage to tell me something I'd already knew. I wasn't going to make him suffer through that.

Later on that night, Mom came downstairs. I knew when she stepped inside the door that she was pissed.

"I should spank your butt for that." She said.

"For what?" I asked knowing full well what she was talking about.

"You really want to make this worse, don't you?" She yelled. "From now on I'll do the telling and don't you even think of telling your father about Paul. He is only my friend."

"Yeah, whatever, Ma." I was not going to get into it with her today.

"Get upstairs. We have to go to your brother's house."

I don't want to go over there. I don't have anything against my brother, but why do I have to be present for this big announcement? She started this whole mess and I am very sure they can do this without me. I couldn't even remember the last time my parents went to my brother's house and yet when they do go over it's to tell him that they're getting a divorce.

My sweet brother is the oldest of the three of us. He recently turned nineteen. He and Bobbie have been living together for a while and are getting married next year. Bobbie is so cool. It's like having another older sister. I can't believe they had a son last year making me the only thirteen-year old in my class with a nephew.

My parents and brother have been at odds for as long as I can remember. It got so bad a few years ago that my brother moved out. I missed having him at home. My sister and I didn't know what to do with ourselves when he left. There was no one to pick on us or to watch over us when we went outside to play. Anyway, why did we have to go over there at 8:00 o'clock at night and on a school night for me no less?

"Hi, Dad. I didn't know you were home." Tyrone said as he opened the door and gave our father a hug. "How you doing, Ma?"

"Hey, son. I just got in today." Dad replied.

Mom hadn't said a word since we got in the car. She gave Tyrone a stiff nod but didn't speak. If I didn't know any better, I'd say she was looking a little down.

"Well, son, your mother and I came over to say something and I won't try to sugar coat it." My dad said taking a seat on the couch.

I can't believe Daddy just blurted out that he and mom were getting a divorce. I don't want to hear this. And why isn't she saying anything? This was her bright idea anyway. She's just sitting there like nothing is happening. Like this family is not about to fall apart. What is she thinking?

I was standing in the doorway of the kitchen with little Ron in my arms. The entire room was quiet. We were all waiting for my brother's reaction. He did the same thing I did. He asked why. I felt completely awful when my dad said that he couldn't answer that question.

Tyrone stood up and said, "What the hell are you talking about? Mom what is he saying?"

Mom was still quiet. I could understand exactly what my brother was feeling. I assume my dad did too, because there is no way on God's green earth that my dad would let my brother get away with talking to them like that. I couldn't come up with words to comfort him. Bobbie stood up next to him and put an arm around his waist. When my brother started to cry she did too. I put Ron down on a blanket in his play area and started washing the dishes in the sink. I just could not bear to see my brother cry like that. I knew he'd take the news badly but not this bad.

I could hear my parents trying to explain to my brother what they had been trying to tell me earlier. This was a bad situation for every one of us. The only unanswered question was why and if my mom knew the answer to it, she was keeping it to herself. For now I guess we'll just have to wonder. Or at least they will because I already know.

My parents dropped me off at home at around 10:00 p.m. Mom told me to take a bath and go to bed. She and Dad needed time to talk and would be back later. I was half paying attention. I just wanted this whole day to be over.

Teresa had left a note saying that she was in Reno and would be back Thursday or Friday. Mimi was already in bed and who knows where L.J. was. I assumed since Joan and Sheila were not in the room that they'd be out for the night too which was fine with me. I could sleep in little late tomorrow since I wouldn't need the extra time to get Sheila ready.

Once I got in bed I couldn't sleep. Then I heard some one walking around upstairs. Just great! I can't sleep and now some one was walking around in the house. I couldn't have been my parents because they hadn't been gone long enough to discuss buying a dog let alone work out whatever problems they were having. I decided to go investigate and while I was at it get a glass of juice.

The light in the hallway outside my room was off and I know I left it on because it's always so dark down here. I could feel someone standing there. If this was L.J. playing around he was going to get slapped.

"John, that better be you or I'll scream!" I said to the darkness.

Then I heard a laugh and I knew it could only be one person standing there in the dark with me.

"Robert, don't you know you could get hurt like that?" I said.

"Hey, baby. What are you still doing up?" He laughed.

"Robert that is not funny. You scared me." I said. I could tell by the sound of his voice that he was still laughing. "Turn on the light, please."

"No. Why don't you make me?" He said.

"Robert when I find you I am going to slap you." I said to dark.

"Those sound like fighting words to me."

"That is exactly what's going to happen if you don't turn on the light." I can not believe he has me down here playing in the dark.

Just then I felt him touch my ear. "So you do want to play?" I asked.

We started listening to movement and chasing each other around in the dark. My hallway is not your normal size narrow walkway. My room used to be where the garage was so the hall widened once you stepped pass my doorway. Then it expanded into the basement so there was a nice size area to play in.

Robert won. He got close enough to grab me around my waist. We stood there holding each other for a long time. It was quiet and I was simply enjoying his company. He started kissing my neck and then worked his way to my lips.

"Hey, Robert is Shay awake?" John yelled from the top of the stairs.

"Yeah, man. We are on our way up." Robert shouted back.

"Does he know?" I asked Robert. He knew exactly what I was talking about and he nodded yes.

"But don't worry." Robert told me. "John loves you like a sister and he knows that I wouldn't take advantage you."

We went on upstairs. John was still hanging inside the doorway. He hugged me and kissed my forehead. Before he let go he said, "I know that you are smarter then the average thirteen year-old and you are going through a lot right now, but let me know if Robert gets out of hand or if you think you can't handle it. Okay."

I said okay and kissed him on the cheek. Robert was already in the refrigerator so I told him to get me some juice. To my surprise he did.

"Why aren't you in the bed?" John asked.

We all sat around the kitchen table and I told them what happened with my parents and my brother. Of course we all knew that mom was seeing Paul and we all agreed that she should have waited until she told Dad before she started spending time with Paul.

"I know he's my uncle but he knows he's wrong." L.J. said.

"I agree, but she's wrong too." I said.

Robert held my hand. I know that he's trying to comfort me, but it wasn't helping. Nothing could stop this hurt I was feeling. After a few more minutes of hanging out with the guys and talking about nothing in particular, I heard my mom and dad coming up the front steps so I kissed Robert and headed back to my room.

A few days later I heard mom on the phone with Melissa. I'd heard the story about the divorce so much that it was beginning to sound like a recording. Melissa must have been very upset because mom was crying and this was the first time I'd seen her cry since this whole ordeal began.

Over the course of two weeks, I'd only seen Dad twice. He moved out of Teresa's house the very next day after we'd all gone over to Tyrone's. Mom did tell me that he was staying in San Francisco with a friend of his. He didn't leave a number, so I couldn't call to see if he was okay.

It's December and I am not at all in the Christmas spirit. How can I be when my world is falling apart before my eyes? There is nowhere to turn and no one to turn to. Joann tries to help. She calls more often now just to see how I'm holding up. Mom is back to her old tricks again. I haven't seen her since that day two weeks ago when I heard her on the phone with Melissa.

Today, Dad is picking up my brother, his family and me later on to take us to dinner. I'm a little nervous about this meeting. I really hope Daddy is doing better, but two weeks is not enough time to recover from losing a spouse of fifteen years.

Having dinner with Daddy was very awkward. Tyrone and I were trying to be so careful about what we said which made having a conversation nearly impossible.

"Dad, where are you staying. Can we call you?" Tyrone asked.

"I'm staying at Jerry's house and I'll give you the number before we leave."

My poor daddy. He sounded so dry and stiff. He looked even worse. Anyone could see the pain on his face. I love you, Daddy.

Chapter 4

Moving On and Moving Out

The days following that last dinner with Dad were very dry. I was so alone. My parent hadn't been around at all. My days were now filled with lots of television and sleep. It was Friday night. School's out for Christmas vacation and I was bored stiff. Well, if my mom and dad were going to be off doing their own thing, I decided to spend the holidays with Joann and Mommy. I was in my room packing when Mimi called down to tell me I had a phone call.

I know it's probably just Jo calling to see if I'd left yet.

"Hello." I said picking up the extension in the kitchen.

" Shay? What are you doing?" It was my mother's voice.

"I'm packing. I'm staying at Jo's for the holidays." I said hoping to make her feel guilty for leaving me.

"Well, honey, you can't go. I need you to do something for me."

I know that sound in her voice. She was up to something and she was beating around the bush.

"Why not, mother? You're not going to be here." I snapped back. I was getting more annoyed by the second.

"Well, you're going to spend the holidays with me and I need you to start packing your things. We're moving."

"What? Moving! Where and when! Mom, I really hate it when you drop bombs on me like this."

"Miss Thang, just do what I asked you to do and I'll there soon." Mom said and hung up.

Well, how about that? We're moving. Mom sure knows how to ruin a girl's day. What am I going to tell Jo? I had no idea that Mom was even looking for an apartment. I wonder where it is. Well, now at least I get to have my own room. No more babysitting Sheila and I won't have to live in this zoo. Oh no, but I probably won't be able to see Robert anymore either.

"Jo, I can't come over. My mom just called and said that I need to pack…"

"Pack?" Jo screamed in my ear cutting me off.

"Yes, loud mouth. She said we were moving. Where to? I don't know, but she 's on her way over now to get me."

"I hope you are coming back on this side." Jo said.

"Yeah, that would be nice. We'd be closer and maybe I can stay over during the week." I said.

"Well I'm happy for you. Call me when you get a chance.

"Ok, I will. Ouch!"

"Who are you talking to?" Said the voice that just walked up behind me. I hadn't even heard him come in the front door.

"What's wrong?" Jo asked.

"Oh, nothing Robert just walked in and poked me in the side. I don't know why he's always trying to sneak up on me."

"Robert?" Jo asked.

"Yeessss." I said trying not to blush in front of him.

"I don't want to talk to you anymore." Joann laughed and hung up. She always knows just what to do.

"Hi, Sweetheart." Robert said when I turned to face him.

"Hi!" I said giving him a big hug.

"Is anyone else here?" He asked.

"Just me and Mimi are up here. I think she's in her room and you know where you can find L.J."

"Good. I'm going to John's room so hurry up and come down."

It's a good thing John's room is downstairs too because Robert and I would have been busted a long time ago. Robert was carrying an overnight bag, which usually meant that he and John were going out and he might even come back to stay the night. I wish my mother would have told me what was going on. I am really going to be upset if we move far and I can't see Robert anymore. Before I could get to the bottom of the stairs, Robert was there waiting.

"What took you so long?" He asked.

"I didn't want to look suspicious." I said smiling back at him.

"Come here and give me my hug. I missed you."

"I missed you too, Robert but you just saw me two days ago."

"Two days, too long." He said just before he greeted me again with a kiss.

Robert picked me up and carried me into L.J.'s room. It was the only safe place in the house because no one ever came into the pigsty that L.J. called his living quarters.

"Hey you guys can have my room for a minute. I've got to go upstairs and iron these jeans." John said as he locked and closed his bedroom door.

I lay down on John's bed and Robert lay down next to me. I have long out grown being nervous around Robert. Over the last six weeks or so we've been quietly meeting in my hallway or in John's room. The most he's ever done is kiss me and I am very comfortable with that. I have been around him enough to know that I can trust him to not try anything more than that. Actually, he has never given me a reason to think or feel that I couldn't trust him.

"Are you okay?" He asked.

"Yeah, I'm fine." I said with a sigh.

"I wanted to talk to you about something." Robert said looking directly in my face.

"What? Have you finally found the woman of your dreams and you're leaving me for her?" I laughed. Robert didn't laugh back.

He went on to tell me that he and John were going out to do their "boys" thing tonight. This usually included a first stop at their favorite bar happy hour. They'll shoot some pool and then head off to the club once the evening turned into night. I'd heard some of what goes on during these "boys" nights. I picked up bits and pieces of their stories when they hung out here at the house with some of their friends, Teresa or Mimi. But for some reason, hearing him say these things now and the tone he used bothered me. I think he was getting concerned about my growing feelings for him.

"You know I would never do anything to hurt you, right?"

He asked. "I just want to be totally honest with you."

"Right, I know." I answered. "Robert, I know that you will meet women when you go out. I mean, I know where the line is drawn for us. I just enjoy the time we spend together."

"But you do know that if I did find a steady girlfriend that I'd tell you, right?"

"Of course, I know that and the same goes for me."

"What?" Robert laughed. "Are you telling me you'd date another man?"

"How about another boy?" I laughed. Robert is so silly. "I really don't think there will be any more 'men' in my near future. Let me stick to the games I know."

"Aw! Thanks, honey. Now, what do you have to tell me."

Robert was just as shocked to find out that I was moving. I told him what Mom had told me and that I needed to start packing before she got here. Robert sat on the bed staring at me like I'd told him I was moving to the very Far East. Before John knocked on the door to tell him that it was time to go, Robert told me that he'd miss me. Robert stood up and handed me his business card.

"Both my work and home number are on here. You know you can call me whenever you want." Robert and I never talked on the phone. There was never a reason to. Beside it being too risky, he always seemed to pop up at the house every other day or so.

I nodded and took the card. "John, you bring him back in one piece." I said. Robert kissed my forehead, nose and mouth. "Call me." He whispered and disappeared out the door with John.

It was just after six o'clock so I walked down the hallway to my room to start packing. What I really wanted to do was I go to Joann's. I wasn't' sure how I felt about this moving thing. In an hour, I'd filled two suitcases and one box. I was doing pretty well or at least I thought. I lay down on my bed and tried to imagine what my new room would look like. I must have thought myself right to sleep because the next thing I knew, I opened my eyes to see my mom standing over me.

"I hope you've finished packing." She said

"I am."

"Bring that stuff upstairs so we can load it into the car."

By the time I got up from my bed, Mom had turned to go upstairs. I guess this means she won't be helping me. When I got upstairs to the kitchen, she'd made herself a cup of coffee and she and Teresa were at the table talking. Seeing that my mom wasn't going to be getting up anytime soon, I dragged my things to the car. The car was a mess. It looked like Mom had been sleeping in it. I am starting to get a little excited. I'll have my own room and maybe Mom will let me get my own phone line.

Mom had more stuff at Teresa's than we had room for so we were going to take this load and come back for the rest. On the thirty minute drive to the city, I tried several times to get Mom to tell me something about the new place, but all she kept saying was that I had to wait and see. I was so happy to see that we were going into San Francisco. Now, I could see Joann more often.

Once we got into the city Mom drove to the Mission District and came to a stop in front of this really nice gray, two-story house. Were moving into this house? I couldn't believe it, we were actually moving into a house. I would have been satisfied with a small apartment, but I'm not complaining. When we got out of the car, I noticed that we were about five or six houses away from the corner. Even from this distance and in the near dark I could see that there was a bus stop on the corner. For me, a bus stop this close only meant an easier access to Joann's house. Excitement started to brew again as we headed for our new home.

The house looked like a castle from the outside. Much bigger than the house we'd moved from in Pacifica when my parents decided they were going to save money to buy their own home by moving in with Teresa. Who knows, maybe my mom would get over this divorce thing now. Maybe she and Dad can work things out and she could get rid of that dried up, rusty Paul guy. Maybe he was just a fling that she needed to get out of her system. Maybe she is clearly aware, now, that she is the mother of three and a wife to one and in a new space she can get her head on straight.

Just inside the gate was the front door. Using the little bit of the streetlight that filtered in behind me I could see that just inside the front door was a long row of steps that curved to the left. Mom switched on the light and we started to climb the stairs. At the top of the stairs was a long hallway that went to my left and right.

"Your room is to the left." Mom said when she reached the top of the stairs behind me. "The light is on the wall to your right when you walk in the room."

I turned left, found the switch and flip! Wow! Would you

just look at this? I had a new bedroom set and the room was painted in my favorite color: pink. I dropped my things right there at the door. I turned to go out of the room. I wanted to see the rest of the house. When I looked down the hallway I notice that the house looked like a castle on the inside as well. The ceilings were the tallest I'd ever seen and there was a skylight in the hallway just outside my bedroom. The house is just beautiful.

There were five doors down the left side of the hallway and three doors on the right. Straight-ahead at the end of the hall was another door. Well, let's go explore! I walked to the first open door on the left, found the light switch and flip! It was the living room. After scanning the room for a brief second I noticed something wasn't quite right. This isn't our furniture. It looked rather old and I know Momma hasn't worked that much overtime to afford a house full of new or old/used furniture.

I went to the next door, found the light and flip! This room was an office. Whose, I don't know. There was a small black couch and two brown leather chairs, a desk and an office chair. I know this is not at all any of the furniture my parents put in storage when we left our house in Pacifica. Mom wouldn't have gone out and bought all this furniture new or used when we still had our old furniture in storage. Would she?

"Mom!" I yelled.

"Mommy!" I yelled again when she didn't answer.

"Girl, stop yelling. I'm in here." She finally said.

I followed the sound of her voice down the long hallway to a room with a light already on. Dang it! Here is another room filled with furniture I'd never seen before. This was obviously her bedroom because she was putting her clothes in a drawer on the opposite end of the room.

"Mom, this isn't our furniture." I said.

"I know that." She snapped as she walked out of the room. I followed her down the hall until we came to a stop inside a very large kitchen with carpeted floors.

"Mother, what's going on?" I asked.

"Will you just give me a minute to put this stuff away? There is someone I want you to meet." She answered.

"Wow."

"Shay, just bring up what you can from the car and I'll tell you about it later." She said. I'd dragged almost all of the stuff from the car just inside the small hall way downstairs before Mom decided to help. I know one thing, I have to find a phone and call Joann soon. She is not going to believe this either. I was nice and tired by the time we finished with the first load and we still had to go back to Teresa's to get the rest of Mom's things, but she said we could do it another day. Thank Goodness!

I found a comfortable spot on my bed to lay down when Mom came in and said we had one more thing to do. Here it is 9:30 at night and she wants to go back out. I hope we are eating because now that I think about it, I hadn't eaten since that sandwich I'd made at lunchtime.

We hadn't driven very far when Mom stopped in front of a pizza place. Good! I'm starving. The least she could do was feed me after the way she worked my little butt this evening. Let me tell you, when we walked into that place I wanted to scream. I could not believe my mother set me up like this.

Paul was sitting in a small booth in the back of the restaurant. Why was he here? I didn't really feel much like being social. I hope she's not expecting me to be nice to him and I don't want to hear anything either of them has to say. I do not like this at all.

"What is he doing here?" I asked Mom as we made our way to the table.

"Sit down and shut up." Mom said back to me.

"Hi, Florine." He said to my mom. "How are you doing? It is Shay, right?"

"Yeah, sure." I said. He could call me whatever he wanted as long as he didn't call me his friend.

"Well, Shay, your mother and I brought you here to talk to you about a few things. So how do you like your new room? We tried to make it the way you would have wanted it."

"What? What are you talking about? What we? What do you care about my room?" I asked. Now he's done it. I've lost my appetite. Paul went on to tell me how he and my mother had fallen in love and that eventually they'd get married. But for now they wanted to be with each other and they did not want me to feel left out, therefore they decided I would be better off living with them in San Francisco than at Teresa's.

When the pizza came I had lost all hope of regaining any feeling for food. They both make me so sick. All the while Paul talked, Mom kept asking if I had any questions. Of course, I had questions. There were a million questions swarming around in my head. I just couldn't decide which one to ask first. Like, what about my dad. Where did he fit in this homely little nest they've decided to create? After all, my mother is still married to him.

What could Florine possibly be thinking? Not to mention, no one bothered to ask me what I thought about any of this. No,

I don't want my parents to divorce and I sure as hell don't want to live with Paul, how about that? I really need to get home and call Joann. She'll know what to do. She and Mommy are good at this sort of thing. Lord knows they've gotten me out of other scrapes with my mother. None this bad, though.

I can chalk this up as being, so far, one of the worst nights of my life. I went straight to bed when we got back to Paul's house. Paul returned to his night job and I was glad about that. I couldn't take another blow tonight. I didn't fall asleep immediately. I just couldn't get over the fact that it was only a few weeks ago that my parents announced to the family their plans to divorce. If time would slow down just a little so that I can get my mind in order. No joke, Paul looked old enough to be my mother's father and my grandfather. I have no idea what she sees in him. And my poor dad. My heart was breaking and there was nothing I could do to stop it.

I woke up the next morning hoping it had all been just a bad dream. I slowly peeled my eyes open to find myself still in Paul's house. Okay, this is not my bed, not my room and definitely not my house! I opened my door and peered down the hall. I walked down the hallway and I heard Mom and Paul talking in their room. I remembered seeing a phone in the office near my room. I made a bee line to the phone. I never knew I could dial that fast.

"Joann, you will never guess what happened." I said when I heard her pick up on the other end.

"Shay, slow down. How am I supposed to guess when you're going 90 miles an hour?" She laughed. I didn't.

Slowing down just a bit, I told Joann about last night. She

sat quietly listening, but I didn't want to stay on the line too long in case my mom came down to check on me.

"Look, I'll see if I can come over later since we are in the city now."

"Okay and Shay try not to worry. I know a lot is happening to you right now, but try to take it easy. You're the only best friend I've got."

"I love you, Jo."

"I love you too. See ya later."

"Bye."

Mom agreed to let me stay at Joann's house as long as I promised to be back by Wednesday night, which was Christmas Eve. That was all I needed to hear. I threw a couple of outfits in a bag and headed for the bus stop. Thirty minutes and one bus transfer later I was sitting with Joann on Mommy's bed. We talked for what seemed like hours. I told her all that had happened over the last week and again what happened last night. Jo understood me better than anyone that's why she's my best friend.

A couple of days at Jo's were exactly what I needed. When I got home late Wednesday, Mom and Paul were in the living room sitting in front of a pretty big fire that they had grown in the fireplace. I sat in a chair opposite them and listened as they told me some of the things I'd have to give up now that Mom and I had permanently moved to San Francisco.

One thing that is staying the same is my school. I don't have to transfer to a new school in the city just yet. I would however, have to transfer next year when I enter high school. Getting to school in the mornings was going to be a drag though. I'll have to get up extra early in order to catch the two buses and train that would get me to school on time.

I decided I was going to be on my best behavior the remainder of Christmas break and, hopefully, I could keep the streak going after that. Even though I felt I was letting my dad down, I had to admit my mom did look happy and who am I to ruin that for her. I'll be a big girl for her. I love both my parents, but I can't control what they do. They have lives of their own too. No one says that I have to like the decisions they make. I know that I'll just have to adjust to my new situation. That's what Mommy had told me and I think that is the best advice she could have given me.

Christmas morning was not like any of the others I'd been through. There was no one at home but Mom, Paul and me. After we exchanged the few gifts that were under the tree, Mom cooked a big breakfast. We sat at the table in complete silence. No one said a word. We each tended to the food on our plates. This is so sad. As soon as I took my last bite I asked Mom if I could be excused and I went to my room. As it turns out, I was in my room for the rest of the day, except once, when I called Joann.

Lying on my bed, I remembered all the previous Christmases with my family. Right after Thanksgiving Mom would put up the tree and lots of lights. Our tree would be over run with presents. Not that all of them were for us. My parents would always get things for family and friends. By mid afternoon the house would be packed with people; my mom's friends, my dad's friends, my brother and sister's friend's and my friends. Family members we hadn't seen since the last big dinner party my parents had. I am going to miss those parties. Oh well, I guess it never hurts to try something new.

Monday morning, following New Year's Day, I was up and out the door before my mom's alarm went off. It was still dark out and the weirdoes were still hanging around the bus stop. I hate being out this early. When I got to school it was 7:30 a.m. Since school didn't start until 8:15 a.m., I decided to walk down the block to McDonald's.

Mickey D's was a little on the crowded side when I walked in. Some guy standing in front of me in line noticed my uniform and asked if I'd like to go ahead of him and so that I wouldn't be late for class. I said "no thanks", but he kept pushing the issue.

"It's really no problem. I wouldn't want you to be late on the count of me." He said.

I had to laugh because it was really not that serious. "Well, if you insist." I said.

"Do you go to that school on the corner?" He asked.

Okay, he thinks it's cool to talk and now I need to get rid of him.

"Yes." I said rolling my neck and my eyes. I ordered my breakfast and was ready to go.

"Hey, I'm going that way. Mind if I walk with you?"

I stopped at the doorway of the restaurant and turned to look at him. Grandma always told me to be careful of strangers. Before I could think of a snappy come back, he'd gotten his food and was coming my way.

"You're not an ax murderer, are you? If you are, remember all these people have seen you with me." I said.

He laughed and opened the door for me. As it turns out his

name was Michael Ford and he was on his way to work at the loading dock in Alameda. He lived on the same block as Teresa.

"Looks like this is your stop." Michael said when we reached the entrance to my school.

"Hey and what do you know, I still have six minutes to spare." I replied.

Michael and I said our good byes so that he could get to work and I could get to class. He gave me his phone number and within a few minutes he disappeared around the corner.

Chapter 5

And Then Some

My life is beginning to run in the same old routines. During the week I go to school and spend the evenings on the phone. My room has become my safe place. The only thing that makes me leave my space is my mom calling to me from down the hall or I need the bathroom. My new living arrangements aren't working at all. My mom and I argue just about every day and the strangest thing is that we argue over nothing and everything at the same time. She is becoming less like my mom and more like a warden which is precisely why I haven't been to Jo's in about a month.

Mom wants me to spend more time with her and Paul on the weekends. She feels we need the time to bond as a family. No matter what she says or does, the three of us together will never be a family. One night I overheard Paul telling my mom that he didn't like kids which was why he didn't have any. Mom told him that he would just have to get used to me. Since then I've stopped going out of my way to be nice to him. The feeling is mutual.

Living here has been no picnic. I've tried to talk to my

mom, but she spends all of her spare time with Paul. When I do happen to catch her alone she rags on me about being in the way. Not a week goes by that I don't hear the words, 'if you could just go live with your dad'. It's not my fault that I was born. She should let me stay at Joann's and that way all three of us will be happy. Steering clear of her heat when I come home is my main objective. I guess that's why I've become accustomed to sleep. If you didn't know any better, one would think I was pregnant as much as I sleep these days.

My phone time was split between Jo, Michael and Robert. I'd meet Michael for a late lunch a few times a week after school and Robert picked me up from school as often as he could. The three of them have been great friends to me. I know I gripe a lot about my home life, but they never complain they just listen until I get tired of talking.

Nothing serious has ever come up between Michael and me. He's become a close friend. and that is a comfortable place for me right now. Although, he is just as cute as he can be. Robert still has my heart. Our relationship has not moved past the occasional hug or kiss. I enjoy his company. In a good way, he forces me to be mature and pushes me to look at my life in a different way.

Although I do not like school much, it has become a part of my new escape. If I can't go to Jo's then school is all I have. Whenever there is an opportunity to for me to volunteer for afterschool tutoring, I make a beeline to get a permission slip from my teacher. I'll do anything to stay out of this house.

"Shay, I heard what you said and no, you cannot stay at

Joann's house this weekend." Mom said.

"Mom, why not? I'm just going to spend the weekend in my room." I said trying to stand my ground.

"You are a part of this family whether you like it or not. You and Paul are going to learn to get along if it kills me. That means you are going to be here this weekend."

"Mom, I don't like being here. Paul acts funny around me. He hates to see me coming when you're at home and then when you go to work he acts like I'm his best friend. And another thing I wish you would tell him to stop hugging me and kissing my forehead. He's such a faker and I hate it." There, I said it.

"Aeysha, you are being ridiculous. Give him a chance and you'll see that he's just trying to be nice to you. You are such a brat and that's your father's fault."

Yeah, right. This conversation was going nowhere fast, so I headed to my corner of the house. I called Jo to tell her the bad news. She was just as upset as I was about the weekend. We could have had a nice three-day weekend since there is a long gap between this holiday in February and the next one coming in April. If I leave it up to my mom, I'll never see Jo again. We haven't been to church in weeks, so I haven't even been able to see my best friend on Sundays.

Mom and Paul had a nice little weekend planned for me. Saturday, they went car shopping while I stayed at home cleaning my room. They thought of me long enough to stop by a give me money to order in and then off they went in Mom's new fire red Mustang. Paul is very good at buying my mother things and she is so spoiled. On all the shopping sprees they have gone on to Macy's or her personal favorite, I. Magnin, not once have they thought to bring a thing back for me.

I don't care if I never have another three-day weekend this year. I am bored out of my mind. Sunday went by very slow. Mom and Paul stayed in their room all day. I even got up early and asked her to take me to church, but she said that she was too tired.

By noon I had had enough, I walked to the bus stop, hopped on the Number 17 to Mission Street and found the Blockbuster my mom was always passing in the car. I had borrowed my mom's rental card a long time ago and since she never asked for it, I didn't volunteer to give it back. I rented a couple of my favorite old movies and headed for the Punjab Chinese restaurant for an order of beef and broccoli over rice.

I had been gone for about an hour and a half. When I got back home the door to Mom and Paul's room was still closed. When my mother finally got up about thirty minutes later, she found me sitting in the middle of my room staring at the television and stuffing my face. I had spread a blanket out on the floor and made myself comfortable.

"I didn't know you left the house." She said from my doorway.

"I was bored Mom. So, I rented these movies and got something to eat." I replied.

"What are you eating?" Mom asked sitting on the floor next to me. Before I could answer she took the fork out of my hand for a taste. "That's pretty good. Where'd you get it?"

"From the restaurant on the corner."

"Oh. Hey, maybe we can all go there one day this week."

"No thanks, Mom." I said.

"Shay, why are you so distant? I just want to spend time with you."

"Mom I don't mind you spending time with me. It's Paul that I don't care to be around. If you want to spend time with me try doing it without including him." I said.

"Aeysha, you are impossible. All you care about is yourself." With that Mom left the room. At least I didn't have to endure a lecture this time. I am so sick of arguing with her; she doesn't listen to me anyway.

On Monday, Mom had to work and she asked me to let Paul know when I was leaving the house and not to pull a disappearing act. Ha, I was not telling his old behind anything. Serves him right, if he wants to sleep all day, then who am I to disturb him? What can he do besides tell my mom that I left? He is not my father therefore; he can't really do anything but tell and I will just deal with my consequence.

When I got out of bed around 9:30 a.m. I was already planning my escape. I had gotten in the shower and was putting on my jacket when I turned to see Paul standing in my doorway.

"How about you and me going to the mall?" He asked.

"Why?"

"Well, I know you wear a uniform to school, but I'm sure you could use some weekend clothes and maybe a couple of dresses for church. So how about it?" He said.

I thought about his suggestion. It was just this past Saturday that I was complaining that he and my mom never thought to bring me anything when they went shopping. Here was an opportunity to get a few things for myself.

"Why not. Let's go." I said. Now he was speaking my

language and I'll try to be nice.

Paul let me go into as many stores as I wanted. He just kept whipping out that little gold card like it was nothing. I had gotten more than I could carry so Paul took my bags out to the car while I tried on shoes. This was fun and better than I thought it would be. I had never been on a no limit-shopping spree before. I'm glad he didn't try to talk to me much. He just let me shop while he sort of stood back. About halfway through the afternoon, I started to think that maybe I could try to be nicer to Paul. I mean really, he was putting forth a very good effort to make me feel comfortable.

It was still a little early when we got home, and I was dead tired from all the walking and stuffed from the buffet we had at Sizzler's. I was going to call Joann but decided to lay down and sleep off some of this food. Boy, was I feeling fat.

"What the hell are you doing?" I yelled at Paul when I opened my eyes. What the hell, am I still sleeping? When I was able to focus my eyes, Paul was sitting on my bed pulling on my shirt. Before I could make a move, he was on top of me tearing at my clothes. He'd pinned my arms under his knees and had his entire weight on pelvic area. I was screaming at him and struggling to get my arms free.

"Get the hell off me you jerk!" I yelled. Maybe I wasn't screaming loud enough. Maybe the people outside couldn't hear me and wouldn't call the police. "Help! Somebody help me!!!!" I screamed as loud as I could. But he wouldn't stop. I yelled until my throat hurt and I couldn't scream anymore.

I felt his hands all over me. I could feel his wet mouth kissing my face and neck. My mind is going in circles and I don't know what to do. The only sounds in the room were of his heavy breathing and the tearing of my shirt. As he started pulling on my jeans I knew I was in trouble and I started crying.

I begged him to stop and I even apologized for being so mean to him. I promised not to tell if he stopped. Nothing worked. He just kept going as if I weren't even there. Paul pulled so hard on my bra that it ripped completely off my body. With his hand inside my pants he proceeded to licking and kissing my breasts.

I started thinking that I can't let him do this. I am literally going to have to fight for my life. I wriggled and struggled as hard as I could until I got one of my arms free. I hit Paul as hard as I could and when he shifted his weight, I kneed him in the groin. He rolled off the bed and onto the floor.

"You little bitch!" He yelled.

My next thought was of my mom. I ran to the kitchen and locked the door behind me. Thank God this kitchen had a door. I reached for the phone and dialed Mom's work number as fast as I could. Just as the phone started to ring at her job, Paul snatched the door open. He hit the left side of my face so hard I was sure he'd broken my jaw. My face burned with pain as I hit the floor.

"Who the fuck you calling bitch?" He said sitting on top of me again. I crossed my arms over my face, but I could still feel some of the blows he was trying so hard to deliver to my face and chest area. We wrestled on the floor for what seemed like hours. The phone was the only thing that saved me. It had fallen on the floor and I was able to reach. When I did I let Paul have it good right across the left side of his face. Then, I just started swinging. I didn't care which part of him I hit, I just kept swinging my arms.

When he seemed more focused on protecting himself, I dropped the phone and ran back down the hall. I locked myself in my room. Then began stacking every piece of furniture I could move behind the door. Thank God Mom listened to me and put a phone in my room. I dialed Mom's work number again. When the operator picked up I told her it was an emergency and that I needed my mom right away.

While I waited on hold for them to page my mom in the warehouse, Paul was banging on my door. "Open this damn door!" He kept yelling.

"I'm on the phone with my mom right now and as soon as she gets here she is pressing charges against you! Stupid idiot!"

"Shay, who are you talking to?" Mom asked when she got on the line.

"Paul! Mom you have to come home right now!" I screamed.

"Aeysha, what is that banging? What's going on!"

"Mom, that's Paul. He's trying to get into my room! I just need you to come get me now!"

"Shay, stop yelling! Let me talk to Paul."

"No, Ma! He's not coming in here!"

"Shay what have you done now? I'm on my way." Before I could tell Mom to hurry she'd already hung up.

I yelled to Paul that Mom was on her way home and that's when the banging stopped. My heart was pounding so fast and the tears were come down like rain. My whole body was shaking and felt so hot. I felt what seemed like tiny needles sticking me all up and down my arms and legs. I tried to take a few deep breaths and shake out my arms, but there was nothing I could do to control it.

I looked down at myself and that's when I really understood what had happened to me. I walked over to the mirror to see if my face looked as bad as it felt. To my surprise it looked worse. The swelling had started around both my eyes and lips. I had scratches on my forehead and right cheek that I must have gotten during the scuffle in the kitchen.

I sat down in the chair next to my window to try to calm my body. The longer I stared at myself in that mirror the worse I felt. I didn't see Mom pull up, but about thirty minutes after she hung up I heard her outside my door talking to Paul. He must have met her at the top of the stairs to get to her before she got to me. I couldn't make out what they were saying, and I didn't care. I stayed exactly how Paul had left me; torn shirt, beaten and all. I wanted my mom to see what kind of pervert she had me living with. With this revelation, I know we are going to be out of here tonight!

"Aeysha, open the door, please." Mom's voice was calm and steady as if she was unsure of what she'd find on the other side.

"Mom, I'm not coming to that door if Paul is out there." I said.

"I can't help you if you don't open the door. I just need to find out what's going on. Paul has already told me his side now I want to here from you. Honey, open the door."

Why is she talking to me like I've lost my natural mind? "Mom, I'm going to open the door, but Paul better not be with you." I opened the door and sure enough Paul was standing right there with my mom. Within a split second I shut and locked the door again. There was no way I was letting that maniac in my room. I don't care that Mom is here. She is so weak when it comes to him. Then my next thought turned to what I'd seen Paul wearing in the brief second I'd seen him at the door. He was not wearing what he'd had on when we go home from the mall. He was not in the clothes he'd assaulted me in. He had the nerve to change his clothes.

From my thoughts I heard Mom's calm, soft and very weird voice at my door again asking me to open the door so that she could talk to me. I had no choice but to open the door. We needed to get this done and over with. I was ready to pack and get out of this house with the quickness. I didn't care if we ended up back at Theresa's. I just wanted out of this house!

"Okay, now I just want you to tell me what happened?" Mom said as she walked slowly over to where I was standing.

"First, you can get that asshole out of this room." I said.

"Shay, watch your mouth. I cannot believe you. Didn't Paul take you shopping today?" She responded.

"Shopping!? Is that what you are worried about!?" I screamed. "Look at me, Mom! Do you think I got this beating while shopping?"

"I guess this is my fault. I should have known better than to bring you here. Paul tried to warn me about you, but I wouldn't listen. How dare you throw yourself at a grown man, Aeysha!"

I was stunned. Maybe she wasn't quite understanding.

"And look at you." She continued. "What in the hell happened to your clothes? Cover up!"

"Mom! Look at my face! I didn't throw myself at anyone. What in the world are you saying?"

Before I could stop myself, I got right in her face and told her exactly what went on and exactly what Paul had done to me. Paul didn't say a word. When I was done breaking it down for Mom, I looked him right in the eye. He had this smirk on his face that really made me want to leap over my mom and hurt him bad. Mom sat on my bed in silence. I think the picture I had just painted was making sense to her now. I know she is in shock, but I was calm enough now to think clearly so I decided to help her out a little.

Kneeling in front of her, I asked, "now can we call the police?"

"What? Call the police for what. Shay we are going to get to the bottom of this. There is no need to call the police." She said me.

"He raped me, Mom! Look at me! I did not do this to myself." I said.

Mom looked at Paul who was now leaning on my dresser. "Did you touch her?" She asked him.

Paul's facial expression never changed. He looked directly at Mom and said, "No. You know that I would never harm her. She's as much my daughter as she is yours. I told you she was having a hard time dealing with us being together and she'd do anything to stop it."

What the hell is he talking about? "Get the hell out of my room you lying pervert! Get out!" I said.

"Shay, I really can't believe you'd go out of your way to hurt me like this. Why would you lie about something like that?" Mom said. Hold up. Is she taking his word over mine? And did she just call me a liar? Mom stood, took one last look at me and walked out of my room. Paul smiled and followed.

BASTARD! I slammed the door and locked it behind them. I felt a new wave of warm tears rush down my face. My whole body deflated as I sank to the floor. I heard the door to my mom's room close and so did my heart. Life as I knew it was over. Not only was I raped and assaulted, my mom didn't believe me. I couldn't understand why this was happening to me. What did I ever do to deserve this? I would never intentionally hurt my mom. Yes, I gave her a hard time, but I love her. She was my mom. She gave birth to me. She is always supposed to be on my side, right?

When I stood to look at my face in the mirror, I cried even harder. I looked like a crazy person. My cheek and lips had swollen so badly. I know I needed to put ice on it but that would have to wait because there was no way I was leaving this room. I sat in the corner of my room in the big recliner. There were so many thoughts running through my mind. I needed rest.

A few minutes later I heard Paul closing the front door behind him as he went off to work. I looked out the window and watched him get in his car and drive away. What could my mom possibly see in that jerk? I sat there listening to all the questions running through my head. Of course, I couldn't answer them all but that didn't mean that they'd stop coming.

I wanted Mom to be happy. I really did, but I also didn't want Paul to get away with what he did. How am I supposed to get through what happened? How am I supposed to understand this? By the time my mind was too tired to think any more, it had gotten dark outside and inside my room. I turned on the lamp next to the chair and looked around my room. It looked as empty as I felt.

I found some pajamas and headed for the bathtub. I felt so nasty. I felt surrounded by filth. My clothes were literally stuck to my body from sweat and tears. I had to peel them away from my skin. I turned on only the hot water. My goal was to burn away every part of my skin that his hands had touched. I scrubbed and scrubbed. The more I scrubbed the redder my skin got. I didn't care because I felt as if I couldn't get clean enough.

I gave up only when the hot water finally turned ice cold. I wrapped a towel around my wet hair, put on some clean clothes, but before I walked back to my room I turned in the opposite direction and stopped at my mom's door. I didn't hear a sound. I wondered what she was doing. I wonder if she felt as defeated as I did.

I turned on the television, sat on the bed and towel dried my hair. I think the news was on, but I couldn't be positive. I just wanted some noise to take away the events of the day that kept playing over and over in my mind. The pictures of what happened never stopped flashing in my head and I knew no matter how much or how long I'd scrub his touch would forever be embedded in my flesh.

As the night went on, my thoughts slowly trailed back to the summer and fall I'd spent at my grandmother's home a year ago. I had never told a soul about the nights my uncle would come into my room. When I left Alabama I thought I could leave all of that behind me. I didn't mention what happened because I was scared. My uncle told me it was my fault and that my mom would be mad if I told.

When Paul came into my room today and tried to have sex with me, I didn't know if it was my fault or not, but I couldn't let them keep doing this to me. I did do the right thing, didn't I?

"Aeysha, are you awake?" A voice on the other side of my door asked.

I didn't answer hoping whoever it was would go away. But along with the questions were a series of non-stop knocks. Then I recognized the voice.

"Shay, let me in." Teresa said.

I let her in and walked over to my recliner.

"I think we need to talk." She said.

"I don't. I have nothing to say." I snapped.

"Your mom called and said that some really disturbing things went on today. Do you want to tell me what happened?" She asked.

"No! I told you that I have nothing to say. Teresa, could you please just leave me alone?"

"Look you can pretend to be as mad as you like, but your mother thinks you are lying and I am beginning to feel the same way! We just want you to tell the truth. Your mom and Paul are getting together and getting married soon whether you like it or not."

"Is that what you think this is about? I could give a damn about what my mother and Paul do. The fact of the matter is that Paul tried to rape me today and if I hadn't had sense enough to protect myself he might have succeeded. You can think what you like, but you are not me and the only reason I haven't called the police is because of my mother!"

"Well let me tell you this Shay, I have known Paul for nearly

30 years. He and his first wife practically raised Mimi. I have never heard anything so absurd."

"Whatever. Like I said think what you want. I'm sure you can show yourself out of my room." I said turning my attention back to the television.

As she stood up to leave, she turned to me and said something I'll never forget; "God doesn't like liars!"

Right at that moment I knew life would never be the same. As of now, it seemed no one was going to believe me. I'd hate for anyone to think that I would actually make up such a thing.

The rest of that week I stayed at home to let my face heal. It was a good thing I had saved some money because I had to eat out every day. Mom wouldn't even look at me. The house was silent except for the times Mom and Paul talked. Maybe Mom could forget what happened, but I wasn't letting him off that easy. I stayed in my room day and night. The only times I set foot outside my door was to leave the house or to use the bathroom.

I might have run into them once that whole week. Mom didn't care if I was coming or going as long as I stayed out of their way. When Mom left for work in the mornings I'd lock my bedroom door and stay there until 4:00 p.m. when Paul left for work. What a way to live.

The following Monday I left the house at 5:30 a.m. I knew it was too early for me to be going to school, but I figured I'd treat myself to breakfast at Mickey D's and get my thoughts together for school. As I walked towards the restaurant I thought I heard someone calling my name. I turned to see Michael coming down the street.

"Long time, no see stranger." Michael said as he stepped up to hug me.

"Hey, how have you been?" I said squeezing him back.

"Why are you out so early this morning?"

"I am treating myself to a sit down breakfast this morning."

"Mind if I join you? I have a few minutes to spare."

Michael and I walked together, ordered and sat down. We talked for about twenty minutes when Michael realized he'd be late for work if he didn't get going. He kissed my cheek and said he would call later so that we could do this again. I'd learned that Michael was 18 years old. He worked as a computer data clerk during the day and took classes at the community college at night.

He didn't bother to ask my age and I didn't volunteer. I'm sure he has some idea since the school that I go to only goes to the eighth grade.

It was about 7:45 a.m. when I got to the gate at my school. I was about to go in when I heard Teresa yelling my name from across the street. My school is just a little too close to her house. When I got to her house she told me my mom was on the phone.

"What the hell do you think you are doing?" My mom said when I picked up the phone.

"Excuse me? You don't say a word to me all week now you want to know what I'm doing?" I shot back.

"Look little girl, I am still your mother. From now on I suggest you let someone know when you are leaving this house. By the way Paul is going to be picking you up from school today." She said.

"Mom, I'll take the bus like I always do. I don't want him

near me!"

"You heard what I said. Just be ready to go when he gets there." She said her final words and then hung up the phone.

I walked out of the house without a word to anyone and headed to school. Obviously, Mom was not listening to me. I could already see that today wasn't going to be my day. I dreaded school. Shawna tried to talk to me, but eventually gave up when I didn't return her enthusiasm about the date she was going on Friday. I feel like I am losing my mind and I do not want to deal with Paul today or any other day.

Sure enough, Paul was waiting outside the gate when I stepped out of the building.

"Hey! Ready to go?" He asked with a smile.

"I'm not going any where with you." I said. The smirk fell from his face.

"Look I did not drive all the way over here to listen to your bull. Now get your butt in this car." He snapped.

"No!" I lowered my voice and continued, "I told you once already and if you don't leave I'll scream." Then I smiled. As I turned to walk away Paul reached out and grabbed my arm.

"I am in no mood for your mess, Shay. Now get your ass in the car or I'll tell your mother." He whispered.

So now he wants to play games. Fine, obviously he doesn't know me very well. I spit in his face, jerk my arm away and walked to the bus stop.

"SHAY! Get back here." He yelled. Everyone within hearing distance turned to see what was going.

I never turned around. I had to laugh to myself because there was no way I was putting up with this mess. I'm not taking it from Mom and especially not from Paul. When I sat down on the bench at the bus stop, I was still fuming. I really don't know who he thinks he is. For one he's not my father and then he tries to make a whore out of me and lies about it when he's busted. I see I'm going to have to protect myself at all costs.

I kept hearing a car horn blowing but was afraid to look thinking it was Paul. Since whoever it was seemed as if they weren't going to give up, I set myself with the meanest frown, looked toward the sound and my eyes found Robert sitting in his car. As soon as I saw him my face softened. I didn't hesitate one moment to jump up and run to him.

"Hey, what's going on? I just saw what happened between you and Paul. Want to talk about it?" Robert asked. "Get in."

"Where are you going." I asked taking my place in the passenger seat.

"I was trying to surprise you by picking you up today. I was standing in front of Teresa's talking to L.J. when we saw Paul yelling at you." He said.

"I have no idea what to do." I said. "I can't tell if I'm coming or going."

Robert reached over, squeezed my hand and told me that I'd be okay. Instead of going straight to home, Robert and I stopped at a small café on Mission St. in downtown San Francisco. Robert ordered a cup of coffee for himself and a hot chocolate for me. We took a seat next to the window. Robert listened quietly as I rattled on and on about my life at home. When I was finished, tears had found their way into my eyes.

Robert held my hands and softly reassured me that life wasn't going to always seem so bad. I wanted to tell him the worst part of all; the incident with Paul but I fought the urge. There was no way I'd tell anyone else before I told Joann.

The wind was starting to pick up when we finally stepped outside the café. Robert really knows how to show a girl a good time. I was feeling a little better until we were near Paul's house. I asked Robert to drop me of on the corner because I wasn't sure if my mom was home and I didn't want her to see him with me.

Before I could get in the house good, Mom was at the bottom of the stairs and in my face. The next thing I knew she'd pulled a belt out of no where and was all over me. That was the first time my mother and I ever physically fought. Surely it would be the last. I love my mom, but she lost my respect when she chose Paul over me. With all the anger I felt inside, I pushed her off me. She fell backward into the front door. Breathing heavily, I told her not to ever touch me again. Mom sat stunned as I turned, went up the stairs and locked myself in my room.

Chapter 6

Change Is Good

It was Friday afternoon and here I am about to walk down the aisle to receive my diploma. All I can think is that it's too bad that it's only from junior high and I can't wait for this day to be over. In all of two days I will be boarding a plane bound for Alabama. I can get away from Mom, Paul and their little love nest. My uncle left my grandmother's last month headed for the Army. With any luck, he will be away long enough for me to finish high school and be off at college.

I was both apprehensive and excited about going back to Alabama. However, I figured as long as my uncle was away, I'd be safe. Since my "incident" with Paul, I had been thinking of a way to get away from both him and my mom. I know that I'm going to miss Joann, Robert and Michael a lot, but this was something I just had to do. The past four and half months have been pure torture. When I wasn't arguing with one of them the house was in complete silence.

I practically lived at Joann's house now. I just couldn't stand being around those two. Half of the time I didn't even bother to ask if I could go. I'd just pack a bag, get on the bus and call her when I arrived. Of course, she'd get upset and yell, but she never drove over to get me, so I figured she was only putting on a show. For who, I don't know. I refused to be nice to Paul and Paul was taking it for everything it was worth. He seemed to like the distance he'd put between my mom and me. Even after all that was going on, they were still talking about marriage.

I lied to Dad and told him that I just wanted to visit grandma for the summer. I had every intention on staying more than that. When I told him that Mom had said that I couldn't go he jumped at the opportunity to piss her off. He didn't hesitate to send me the money.

Dad Federal Expressed the money to Mommy's house so that my mom wouldn't find out what I was up to. Jo and I called the airline to make the reservations. I gave Mommy half the money that was supposed to be for a round trip ticket and she charged the one-way fare on her credit card. The rest of the money would be pocket money for my trip. Only Joann knew that I wasn't planning to come back. We didn't want to tell Mommy out of fear that if she knew the truth, she'd try to convince me to return or tell my mom.

I'm almost positive that if Mommy had known I wasn't planning on returning at the end of the summer, she would have never purchased my ticket. I didn't want to lie to her, but I just had to get away from my mom.

It wasn't until a week before graduation that I told Mom I was leaving. After she finished yelling, I told her it would only be for the summer and she'd have me back in no time to yell at. Then good old Paul said that it would be best for all of us if I went away for a little while. How about that?

I searched the crowd at the graduation for my dad. He said that he'd try to make it. I sent an invitation to Seattle over a month ago and I know he should have gotten it by now, but still I didn't see him in the crowd. I could see Michael. Mom, Paul, and Tyrone had found seats next to each other. I'm glad Tyrone took the time to come. I hadn't seen him in a long while. He and Mom had been on the outs since she made the divorce announcement. Tyrone like Paul about as much as I did. Hopefully, all three of them would remain civil today.

The ceremony lasted about forty-five minutes. The Catholic school I attended was small and therefore my "graduating" class was only twelve students. When the ceremony ended, Michael was the first person I was able to make eye contact with and I had to fight my way through the small crowd to get to him.

"Michael! I'm glad you made it." I said hugging him the instant I got to him.

"Hey, you know I wasn't going to miss your big day." He replied handing me a lovely bouquet of flowers, a small box and a card I immediately read:

Best friends are hard to come by.

I'm very glad I found you.

Love, Michael

"Oh, how sweet. Thank you so much." I blushed.

"I'm going to miss seeing you at our spot every week." He said.

"I'll miss you too, but you promised you'd write." I said. I told Michael when we talked on the phone last night about my plans to leave for a while.

"I will. I know you need to go away for yourself but don't

forget me."

"Michael, I wouldn't do that." I said giving him another hug. We must have held on a bit too long because the next voice I heard was my mom's.

"Who is this?" I heard my mom ask from behind me and I could tell by her voice that she was not pleased.

"This is Michael. Michael this is my mom, Florine Noland." I said dryly. I didn't even look Paul's way.

"How are you?" Michael asked extending his hand to shake Mom's.

"Fine, thank you." She replied with much attitude and ignoring his hand.

Michael also noticed mom's attitude, so he said good bye, kissed my cheek and said he'd call later.

After hugging all of my classmates and exchanging addresses, it was time to go. Mom, Paul and Tyrone were waiting in the parking lot near the car when I walked out of the building.

"Congratulations, Sis." Tyrone said while giving me a hug.

"Thanks. Where's Bobbie?" I asked.

"She stayed at home with the baby. He's got a cold."

"Tell her I said hi."

Tyrone handed me a big box, kissed my forehead and turned to leave without another word. I could tell by the look on his face that he was still fighting with his emotions over the divorce. I'm sure seeing Mom with Paul hadn't helped much. I just hope he can find some way through it and not let it tear at him every day. This divorce thing has been hard on all of us kids, but I think it is affecting him a bit more.

On the drive home, all Mom could talk about was Michael.

She wanted to know where we met, how we met and how old he was. I answered as vaguely as I could. Two days left was all I could think about. I was not going to let her ruin my day. It was bad enough that Dad hadn't shown up.

Not five minutes after we were in the house, the doorbell rang. I didn't bother to answer it because all I wanted to do was change my clothes and get out of this house. On my way to the bathroom I stopped to see Mom coming back up the stairs with red roses and a huge white teddy bear.

Even though the envelope was addressed to me, Mom opened it and read aloud, "Congratulations! I hope you have a wonderful day. Love Always, Robert." She looked at me. "Who the hell is Robert and why is he sending you all these damn roses."

"Mom, first of all that was addressed to me. Robert is just a guy I know. I'm sure he sent them because of the graduation. So, could you give them to me please?" I said.

"Look, girl. You better watch your mouth. You are entirely too young to know anybody who could afford to send you not one, but two dozen roses. Shay, I want to know who he is right now and what you did for him to send you these roses!"

"Robert is no one you need to be concerned with and if I'd known he was going to pull a stunt like this I would have told him not to." Now I was yelling. What is her problem anyway?

She started giving me a disgusted look, so I took the gifts from her and headed for my room. Two days! Mom stomped her way into my room and closed the door.

"Do you want to tell me what you are doing with these boys?" She asked in a much softer tone.

"What? Ma, what are you talking about?" I was getting annoyed.

"Shay, are you having sex?"

"You are kidding right?" I had to laugh. "After what happened to me you think I'd want some man touching me?"

"While we are at it let's see what this other gift is from your 'friend'." Mom said grabbing the little box that Michael had given me, which I still had not opened, from my dresser. Before I could say a word, Mom was tearing the paper off of my neatly wrapped gift.

"What are you doing?" I yelled at her.

"I have a right to know what this is." She said popping the top on the box."

"Mother that was a gift for me. Why do you always act like you're interested in my life when nice things happen? If I hadn't gotten any gifts today you'd be locked up in that room with Paul right now."

She pulled out a beautiful charm bracelet. It had the letter M, a small hamburger and what appeared to be French fries hanging from it. I thought it was so neat. I took it from my mother and she read the note Michael had tucked inside the box.

"We can always add to it." She said. Mom was furious at this point. She kept yelling about how I must have been having sex with these boys for them to be giving me such nice gifts. I tried to explain to her that they were neither my boyfriends nor sex partners but merely friends. No matter how many times I said friends she still didn't believe me.

Finally, Paul knocked on the door and asked Mom if she wanted to go to dinner. Of course, she said yes, and I was relieved. As she walked out my door she turned to tell me that we'd talk about this later. Of course, that was the last thing I wanted. As soon as they were out of the driveway I picked up the phone to call Robert.

"Hello." Robert said in his deep baritone voice.

"Hi, Robert. It's yours truly."

"Hey, stranger. Congratulations. You know I would have come, but I didn't want you to get into any trouble."

"Yeah, I know and thank you so much for the roses and bear. Mom nearly died when they were delivered."

"Oh, no. I hope you didn't get into too much trouble. Did she know who they were from?" He asked.

"She actually read the card." I laughed. "But she didn't know that it was you. So, don't worry."

"I hope you were surprised, but I wish I could have brought them by myself." He said softly. "Shay, are you okay."

"Of course. Why?"

"L.J. told me what happened between you and Paul. I'm really sorry. You know you could have called me."

"Robert, I'm fine really. I know that I can call anytime I want, but that was something that I had to deal with alone. It'll take some time before I can fully understand what was going on and why this happened to me."

"Is that the reason you're going away this summer?" He asked.

"Robert, I'm going to be honest with you. That is one reason I'm going away this summer, but I am not coming back any time soon."

"You are kidding right?" He asked with his voice going up

a notch.

"Afraid not, honey. I've had about all that I can take of my parents, this whole divorce thing and especially Paul." I said trying to hold back tears.

"I know and I understand. No matter how long you'll be gone, I will miss you. You call me and let me know if you need anything, okay?"

"I will. I'll let you get back to work and I'll talk to you later."

"Okay. Love you."

"Love you, too. Bye."

I'm sure Teresa told anyone and everyone who would listen about what happened to me. I can only imagine what was said. Neither Teresa nor my mom ever bothered to really talk to me about it. They automatically assumed I was lying and left it alone but not without telling the world first.

Anyway, I spent the rest of the day on the phone. Mom and Paul were gone, and they were the reason I wanted to leave the house to begin with. Jo and I had made plans to get to the mall early the next morning.

Thinking about what clothes I'd need to pack, I looked over at my dresser and noticed that I hadn't opened the box Tyrone gave me. With all of the drama with my mom when we got home, I'd put the box down on the dresser and forgotten about it. Tyrone and Bobbie had given me a stuffed bear holding roses. It was kind of kiddie but cute. I started to place the bear back in the box when I noticed a small white envelope with my name on it at the bottom of the box.

Upon tearing into the envelope, I found three crisp one

hundred-dollar bills and a note from my dad apologizing for missing my graduation. I know that Dad probably didn't come because he didn't want to face Mom and Paul. But regardless of what she's doing, he shouldn't let that come between us. Then again, I'm just a kid so what do I know.

It was getting late and I was getting tired. Mom and Paul were still out so I guess that means I'll have to fend for myself as far as dinner was concerned. I was not in a cooking mood and I didn't want to go out, so my only option was ordering a pizza. I walk into the den to find the phone book and just then my phone started to ring.

"Hello!" I said diving on the bed to catch the phone before my answering machine picked up.

"I just wanted to say good night." Said the voice on the other end.

"I was beginning to think you'd forgotten about me already. I left a message hours ago."

Michael laughed. "No way, baby."

"Thank you for the gift. It is absolutely beautiful." I said.

"You're so very welcome. Just make sure you wear it everyday."

"I will."

"I'll call you tomorrow." Michael said. "Get some sleep."

"Goodnight."

Aw! Michael is so sweet. I dialed the number to Round Tables and ordered a large mushroom, beef and pepperoni pizza. This is mine and Jo's favorite. As I laid across my bed waiting for my dinner, I started thinking about how wrong my mother was about guys.

She's always telling me that guys only wanted one thing from a girl, but I know two guys that have become very good friends of mine and not once did they ever try any thing shady. After all that happened with Paul, s-e-x is the last thing on my mind. If I can help it, I won't be forced into having sex and I most definitely won't be pressured into it. I will do it in my own sweet time.

The doorbell rang and I jumped. I had not realized that I'd been on my bed that long daydreaming about my limited knowledge and understanding of the male species. My pizza was so good and so hot. I got a soda from the kitchen, flipped on my television and devoured four slices of pizza. By the time I started my fifth slice, I was stuffed, feeling very fat and The Cosby Show was going off. I was thinking about taking a shower and calling it a night when the phone rang.

"This better be good." I said into the phone with a little more attitude than I intended.

"Aren't you just a little rude this evening? Think you all that now that you graduated from junior high."

"Melissa?" I said very much surprised. "Why on heaven's earth are you calling me at this hour?"

"I called Mom but no one answered her phone. So I decided to bug you."

"Gee, thanks."

"Where is Mom anyway?"

"Your guess is just as good as mine. They left here hours ago and haven't called."

"You mean to tell me that you are in the house alone at this hour?" Melissa asked.

"Lissa, I'm not a baby. Mom and Paul do their thing and I do mine."

"Yeah, well you know if it were me I would have had to throw a party."

"Melissa, you are too much."

Melissa and I talked for about an hour. She and Aaron, her boyfriend, were going to his family reunion in Mobile, Alabama and wanted to get started early for the long drive. She and Aaron have been together for about three years now.

I told Lissa about my graduation and the nice gifts that I got. We both had to laugh when I told her how Mom overreacted to Michael and Robert's gifts. Melissa knew all about Michael and Robert. In fact, Melissa and Jo were the only ones that could understand how I could be friends and only friends with guys much older than I am. Melissa was the one who was always telling me that I was mature for age and giving me advice on not letting boys talk me into things I wasn't ready for. She was the one who told me about the birds and the bees. She took the time to tell me all there was to know about sex. Thank God I have a great big sister.

Saturday morning, I left my house at 7:00 a.m. I was still waiting at the bus stop at ten minutes after seven when I saw mom and Paul pull into the garage. I did leave her a note this time. I really hope she doesn't send Paul to Mommy's or the mall looking for me.

When I got to Jo's house Mommy had just finished making her big Saturday morning breakfast. Joann was at the table stuffing her face when I stepped into the kitchen.

"Hey, Aeysha, baby." Mommy said to me.

"Hi, Mommy." I said smiling and kissing her cheek.

"Shay, don't just stand there, get a plate. Are you girls coming to the store with me today?" Mommy asked.

Jo nodded while I agreed and reached into the cabinet for a plate. As long as I've known Jo, Mommy has gone to the grocery store every Saturday, without fail. Jo and I loved shopping with Mommy. Not only because she let us pick out whatever we wanted, but because just being around her was nice. Mommy was really down to earth. She wasn't afraid to laugh with us, be silly with us or have tough conversations with us.

After breakfast, we piled into Mommy's car, backed out of the garage and headed to the grocery store. It was still early so the store was not crowded at all. This gave me and Joann the liberty to wonder up and down each aisle, pulling all of our favorites off the shelves.

Back from the grocery store we helped take the bags in and put up food. It was nearly noon when Mommy dropped us off at Brookside Mall. I bought shorts and tops for the hot Alabama sun. Joann bought a Hello Kitty wallet and jacket for these cold California mornings. We both had to get new shoes. We walked to food court to have Round Tables pizza by the slice.

"Hey, girl. What's your name?" Some guy said to Jo while we sat eating our lunch.

"Excuse me?" She said.

"I'm sorry. Let me start over. My name is Cedric and yours?"

"Candice." Joann said and continued to eat.

I let out a little laugh when I heard Jo using her fake name. She and I always used fake names when we were out somewhere. She was Candice and I was Michelle. Cedric tried real hard to get Jo to notice him. He took it upon himself to sit down at our table to continue his conversation with Joann. She said a few words to him but acted very uninterested. Which I'm sure she was. I sat quietly eating my slice and listening to them talk.

That poor guy. When Jo was finished with him he looked defeated. We did learn, however, that he was a freshman at Brookside High and lived in the Summit view area. He was rather cute. Jo took his number when he offered it and said she think about calling. With that, Cedric stood and walked over to join his friends that had been waiting for him.

When Cedric was far from our table and out of our view, we cracked up. Jo knew she was wrong. I was always telling her that whenever she talked to a guy she gave him a true run for his money.

"If guys think they have a shot at even having a phone conversation with me, they need to approach me proper." Jo always said. That's my girl!

We left the mall at around 4 p.m. We were beat, but that little shopping binge was well worth the beating. A forty-five-minute-long bus ride was exactly what my feet and legs needed. Jo and I laughed and talked all the way. I hung out at Jo's house until 7:30 p.m. I knew I needed to get home, but I also didn't want to say good bye to her.

The sun was on it's was down so Mommy decided to drive me home. Despite my note, Mom was very upset when I walked in the door. Mommy even came in to tell her that I was indeed with her and Jo all day, but Mom wasn't trying to hear that. Funny that she hadn't called Mommy's house once to ask if I was there or to yell at me, yet she waits until I arrive home to show out. I was feeling like she needed an excuse to argue with me tonight.

Jo called about an hour later to see if I was still alive. I am certain Mommy filled her in on the drama she witnessed when she got home. I didn't want to talk long because saying good bye was much too hard. I'm going to miss her terribly.

A few minutes after Jo and I hung up the phone started ringing again.

"Hello."

"You don't sound too happy." Michael said.

"Michael, I was waiting for you to call!"

"I just wanted to be the last person you said good bye to." He said.

Michael and I talked until the early morning. We mostly just held the phone in silence. It seemed like his was trying to not let go of me. We talked about everything under the sun and he never once said that he wanted to get off the phone. Time just flew by.

At about 5:15 a.m. I had to say good bye. I still needed to take a bath and do something with this stuff attached to my head. I really wasn't up for a fight with my mother this morning about my leaving. I jumped in the shower and fixed my hair as best I could.

Mom knew what time I was leaving to catch my plane, but still she didn't get up. When she still wasn't up when I came out of the bathroom, I decided not to wake her at all. I made a decision to call a cab. I sat on my bed wondering if my mom would get up and come down the hall to check on me. I had already taken my bags downstairs. So when I heard the cab driver blow his horn, I walked over to my window to wave at the drive to let him know I was on my way down. Shutting my bedroom door, I stood in the hallway listening to the silence that surrounded me. I guess Mom thought if she didn't get up to take me to the airport, then I wouldn't be able to go.

Stepping out in the early morning sunrise, the cab driver looked at me very strangely but took my bags. I'm certain he was wondering if he should let me in his cab.

"So, you're headed to the airport?" He said as he held the door open for me.

"Yes." I replied. My coach and cheer team are waiting for me. We are taking a short trip to Los Angeles to compete in a regional championship.

"Wow! That's pretty cool, young lady! Well, let's get you to the airport."

I'm glad he believed my story. I wanted him to think someone was waiting for me and would notice if I hadn't arrived. The cab driver took me straight to the airport. He asked more questions about my competition and I fed him more highlighted stories. When we pulled to the curb, I saw a white lady standing next to a curbside attendant. I waved to her and thankfully she waved back.

"There's my coach." I said to the driver.

He seemed glad that someone was there waiting for me. He sat my bags on the curb. As I handed him his fare, he waved to the lady too. When he got back in his cab and drove away, I walked into the airport to find my airline and check-in.

Check-in was easier than I thought it would be. I was ready with another story to give the attendant if I was asked why an adult wasn't with me. However, when it was my turn at the counter, I simply handed her the notarized form my dad had signed saying I was traveling alone, my birth certificate, my social security card and my school ID. After printing my ticket, she called over another attendant who walked me to my assigned gate and left me with an attendant there.

I boarded the plane praying that I'd make it to my grandma's house in one piece. As soon as I found my seat, I got a blanket, a pillow and went fast asleep. I have never liked airplanes, but this trip was an important one. Also, I seriously doubt that Mommy would have played any hand in helping me purchase a ticket for a bus ride across the country alone.

"Ladies and gentlemen we will be landing at Meridian International Airport in about 10 minutes. At this time I'll ask that you put your seats and tray tables in the upright position. The time is 4:20 p.m. and the temperature in Mississippi is 95 degrees. This is your captain speaking and thank you for flying Delta Airlines."

I like the sound of that. It looks as if I'll make it after all. I hope things haven't changed much since I was here last summer. Now I'm really starting to feel bad because I didn't keep in touch with anyone. I'm sure I'll be okay, after all I am going to be with the world's greatest grandmother.

Chapter 7

Let the Good Times Roll

Melissa and Aaron are ten minutes picking me up. Sitting in this small airport is miserable. The air conditioner is on, but it is still so hot that I am sweating through my t-shirt. I'd forgotten how hot it is during the summer in Alabama. They better show up soon or I'm calling grandma. They are about the slowest two people…

"There's my little sister." Before I could finish my thought my sister and Aaron were walking into the airport.

"Hi." I said happy to see them. "Aaron, you haven't changed a bit."

"Hey girl, let's get out of here. We have a very long drive ahead of us." Aaron said grabbing my bags.

Melissa put her arms around me and led the way to the car. I was so excited to have my big sister back. The drive to grandma's house was just a little over an hour. For me, the time passed by quickly because Melissa and I didn't stop talking until we pulled into my grandmother's yard. After that drive, I was certain that I was completely caught up on all the latest town gossip.

"There's my baby." Grandma said as I got out of the car. "Come give me a hug girl. Look at you. You're as thin as a carrot. Grandma's gone have to fatten you up." Every time she saw me, she was always threatened to 'fatten me up.'

"Hi, Grandma!" I laughed, wrapped my arms around my grandmother's thin waist and held on for dear life.

Grandma half dragged, and half carried me into the house. I only let go of her to hug the rest of the family and some of my friends who had gathered in my grandmother's living room. Melissa had to have opened her big mouth and told everyone that I was coming back.

You could smell the food my grandmother had cooked a mile away. I was still a little full from the food the served on the airplane, but I'd have no problem making room for hers.

My mother's youngest sister Yolanda still lived at home with my grandmother. We didn't always get along. When I came into the house she gave me a very nasty look and turned away. I never quite understood her negative attitude toward me. Well, she didn't get along with my mother either so maybe she hated me for being a reminder of my mother.

My friends and I flopped down on the couches and chairs in the living room planning what we were going to do my first night back. Chris sat down right next to me and threw his arm around me. Here we go again, I thought. Chris asked me out so many times the last summer I was here that I thought I'd have to choke him.

He never gave up and by the end of the summer it had become our little game. Every couple of weeks or so he'd call and ask me out, I'd say no and then he'd come over and sit out on the porch with me until I had to go in. He's a great guy but not one I'd want to date.

His grandmother and my grandmother were good friends and even though I didn't want him as a boyfriend, he just became part of the crew. All my friends wanted to do was ask me questions about my city life. Stories about my life in California had always fascinated my friends. They seem to think I run into famous people all the time. It's funny. I often reminded them that they watched way too much television and that they need to venture out of this town once in a while.

"Shay, I have someone I want you to meet." Melissa whispered in my ear.

"What?" I asked.

"Just let me know when you are done socializing." Lissa said with a smile.

It was nearly 9:00 p.m. when people started leaving for the night. My friends, my sisters' friends, my grandmothers' friends, seemed to flow in and out of the house for most of the afternoon and evening. Of course, everyone was stuffed from grandma's wonderful dinner. She'd cooked all of my favorites: collard greens, macaroni and cheese, sweet potatoes, hot water corn bread and spaghetti. It was a very good day.

The telephone rang and just then I remembered that I hadn't called my mother to let her know that I'd made it. "Aeysha, the phone's for you." Yolanda yelled from the hallway.

It was Melissa. Wow, that girl is quick. I hadn't even noticed that she'd left the house. She and Aaron were on their way to pick me up and I was to be waiting on the porch for them. I tried to get out of going, but Lissa wasn't hearing it.

"You have the rest of the summer to lay around and sleep. I haven't seen you in over a year and there is much to do before you go back home." Lissa said and hung up the phone.

I sat on the couch next to grandma and waited for Melissa. Grandma said that she had called my mother earlier to let here know that I was safe. She also told me she'd handle my mom this summer and that I was not to worry about a thing.

Grandma knew that adjusting to Mom's relationship with Paul and the divorce was hard on me. She and I decided that I wouldn't spend too much time thinking about that this summer. Now was not the best time to tell her that I was planning on staying. I guess I'll step on that nail when I have to.

"I guess you'd better go before Aaron wakes up the neighbors blowing that horn." Grandma said.

"Thanks for the talk Momma." I said kissing her cheek.

"Shay just so you know, Lissa's curfew is 12:00 a.m. and yours will be 11:00 p.m. Got it?" She said. "I know this is your first night back, but I'll let you stay out tonight with Melissa. Y'all be careful."

Grandma gave me a hug and pushed me out the door. My grandmother is the best, but I knew when she meant business. I was not about to try her on this night or any other night this summer.

"Hi." I said once seated in Aaron's car.

"Shay, that's Tony." Melissa said pointing to the skinny boy that was next to me in the back seat. "Tony, meet my sister, Aeysha."

Now that Melissa was done with the introductions the car was quiet except for the sound of music blaring from the radio.

"Where are we going?" I asked in general.

"Into town." Tony answered staring directly in my face.

Glancing at Tony, I realized he was a little on the cute side. He had big round eyes, but I couldn't see what color they were. He also had a nice smile. Seeing how Aaron and Melissa were in a world of their own that meant I was stuck with Tony. Not quite sure why Melissa felt she needed to introduce us. I'd seen him around town last year when I was here, but he didn't hang out much. I knew he was Aaron's brother.

Through our backseat conversation I learned that Tony was also thirteen and was Aaron's youngest brother. He let me know that Aaron had told him this morning that I was coming. Aaron and Melissa thought it was a good idea for us to hang out tonight.

"You were in a class with me the year I went to school here, right?" I asked.

"Yeah, I was in algebra with you, but you didn't talk to me that much." He said looking down at his hands.

"Sorry." I said tempted to laugh but held back.

"Do you think you might stay for another school term?" Tony asked.

"I don't know. I just want to have a good summer."

I could tell that Tony was just as shy as Aaron and if any conversation was to be made, I was going to have to do most of the work. I was certain we were driving to the town nearest to us, about thirty minutes from where my grandmother lived. At the center of town was a small park. It was well lit, had benches, a play area and a small fountain.

Aaron found a spot near the edge of the park and we all got out. Pretty much everyone from the surrounding smaller towns hung out here. Aaron and Melissa took off walking in one direction while Tony and I found a bench near the fountain. Tony asked if I wanted to get a slice of pizza from the pizza place that was still open across the street from the park, but there was no way I could eat another bite of anything.

Tony and I sat and talked, walked and talked. Despite being very shy, Tony was rather interesting. He enjoyed reading like I did and his favorite flavor of ice cream was vanilla just like mine. By the time we were on our way back home, Tony seem a little less shy and was making me laugh. When we pulled in front of the house he had mustered up enough nerve to ask if he could come by tomorrow. I agreed to let him.

"So how was your date?" Grandma asked with a big grin on her face.

"Ma, what do you know?" I asked her suspiciously. "And it wasn't a date."

"Nothing. I just know that Tony is a nice boy and you need someone nice to hang out with this summer.

"Yeah, right. Besides, I thought I'd hang out with you this summer."

I heard the front door close. Melissa walked into the living room smiling. Don't know why she's smiling so hard and I don't know what Grandma and Lissa are up to, but I'm not going to let them sneak anything passed me.

"Oh, so you do come up for air." I said to Melissa teasing her about Aaron.

"Shut up." She said tossing a pillow at me.

It was great being around my sister again. She and I have always gotten along great. It was real weird not having her at home with me in Cali. If she only knew how much I needed her there.

Lissa and I stayed up talking long after Grandma and Yolanda had gone to bed. Grandma's house was very small. I will never know how she managed to raise nine children in there. What used to be a very small two-bedroom, one bath house was now a three-bedroom, one bath house. About two years ago my mom had the house remodeled and closed in Grandma's back porch. This area now served as my and Melissa's bedroom.

Tony stopped by early Monday afternoon. I had not too long ago gotten up, was still in my pj's and rollers and in desperate need of a bath. I guess I was more tired than I thought. Yesterday had been a very long day. Tony sat quietly in the living room while I got dressed. Melissa stuck her head in the bathroom door and told me to hurry.

"What's the big rush?" I said.

"We are going into town for Momma and she wants us to hurry up and come back." She said leaning the sink. "Tony's coming with us."

"And!" I said to her.

"He told Aaron that he thinks you're nice."

"Lissa what are you getting at? I told you last night I didn't come here to find a boyfriend."

"Aw! Shay, what wrong with a little summer romance?"

"Lissa, not everyone has to have a boyfriend all the time." I said stepping out of the bathtub.

"Shay, look, I know that you're dealing with a lot right now, but don't let Mom's choices ruin your life."

"Thanks, Lissa. Have I told you lately that you are simply

the best?"

Melissa kissed my cheek and said "Enough chit chat. Tony's waiting for you." Then disappeared out the door.

There was still not much to see in downtown Flood, Alabama. We stopped at the drug store to pick up Grandma's medicine and then at Piggly Wiggly on the corner to get the few things she needed for tonight's dinner. Aaron stopped at the hospital on the edge town and we all jumped out of the car again.

"Who are we seeing here?" I asked turning to Tony.

He smiled and said, "my mother."

"What do you mean. Is she sick?"

"No." Tony said laughing. "She works here, and we are bringing her lunch."

Once we were inside the sliding glass doors, a short, round lady walked up to us. When she hugged Melissa, I figured she must be their mother.

"And you must be Shay." She said grabbing my hand.

"How are you?" I asked not knowing what else to say and wondering what Tony could have possibly told her about me in less than twenty-four hours.

"Mom, we've got to go." Aaron said kissing his mom's cheek and handing her a bag which I assumed was her lunch.

Walking back out the sliding glass doors I noticed my sister smiling again with that weird look on her face. When we were nice and comfortably seated in the car, Aaron and Melissa were off in their own conversation, I turned to Tony.

"What could you have told your mom about me after only one date?" I asked.

"Date?" He smiled. "Is that what last night was?"

I laughed because I knew I'd set myself up for that one. "Tony, that is beside the point. What did you tell your mother?"

"I only told her that you seemed nice and that I l...." His voice turned to a whisper.

"What was that?" I said smiling.

"I told her that I like you." He said with his face in his hands.

"Oh! Well that's nice." I said toying with him.

"That's nice?"

"Yes, that's nice."

"I knew I shouldn't have told you."

"Tony, look at me. I was only teasing. I think you're nice too."

"You do?" Tony's eyes brightened.

"Yes."

Chapter 8

Stay for Awhile

Summer had gone by in a flash. I had been spending all my spare time with Tony and I really hadn't thought about home much until Grandma asked me what day my return flight was scheduled for. She and I were sitting in the living room watching TV. Both of us with a large bowl between our legs shelling peas. When I didn't speak right way, my grandmother's hands stop moving. When I told her that I hadn't purchased a round trip ticket and that I wanted to stay in Alabama she nearly lost all control.

"Shay, what do you mean you didn't purchase a round trip ticket and when were you planning to let me in on this little plan of yours."

"I'm sorry, Grandma. I really am." With tears beginning to well up in my eyes, I explained how much I hated living with my mom and Paul. I needed a break from them badly.

"You should have talked to me when you first got here, Aeysha." She was using my given name which meant she was not at all happy with me at the moment. "Does your mom know about this?"

I let my silence speak for me.

After a few days of thinking it over, Grandma called her daughter to let her in on what I'd decided. I thought Mom would have been upset, but she told grandma I could stay as long as I wanted to. But after she hung up the phone, Grandma had the strangest look on her face.

"Shay, where is Lissa? I need to talk to you girls for a minute." Grandma said.

"I think she in the backyard playing basketball. What's the matter? Did something happen to Mom?" I asked. Grandma didn't answer. She walked to the back door and yelled for Melissa to come back to the house.

"Your mother and Paul have decided to get married in April. She wants both of you there." Grandma said once Lissa and I came into the living room.

I was at a loss for words, so Melissa spoke first. "I'm not going." She stated flatly.

"What do you mean you're not going? Your mother is going to send for both of you."

"Well, if we go to the wedding, is she going to let us come back here when it's over?"

"That, I don't have the answer to Shay. I guess you'll have to ask her." Grandma answered.

"I'm with Lissa on this one, Gran. I'm not going either." I said.

Grandma tried to talk us into changing our minds and said that over the next few months we should really think about going. I was more afraid that Mom would try to make us stay. I'm still not sure if I can tolerate being in the same house as Paul.

Now it was really starting to sink in that my parents were going ahead with their separate lives. Dad was on assignment again, so I hadn't spoken to him in over a month. He calls grandma every once in a while, to make sure we are okay and not giving her any trouble. I wonder how he's going to feel about Mom getting married again. Better yet, what brave soul is going to tell him?

Even though I was enjoying my friends in Alabama, I was really missing Joann. We had written to each other over the summer and grandma would let me call her at least once a month as long as I kept up with my chores and stayed out of trouble. I was feeling bad about my decision to stay because this was supposed to be the year that Jo and I were to start school together.

I went outside to find Melissa and shot a few baskets with her. Of course, she did not look at all happy about the recent turn of events happening in our family. I think that out of the three of us, Melissa, was taking our parents' divorce the hardest. She doesn't talk about Mom or Dad at all and if either one of them call she often steers clear of the phone.

"Lissa, you want to tell me what's going on with you?" I asked sinking my fourth basket in a row.

"Look, Shay. I could just care less about what Mom does. I can't believe she's pulling this mess. Where does she get off?"

"I know what you mean, but we don't have to go. Regardless of what we think she's going to marry that asshole."

"Watch your mouth, Shay! Look, it may be easy for you but remember our father is the only father I know. It's bad enough that I never even had a chance to know my biological father.

Now Mom's gone off and left the only father I ever knew. It's not fair, Shay and you know it."

"Lissa, I know it's unfair. You are not the only one losing out here. Dad had been there for all three of us!"

"Girl, you know exactly what I mean. I know that Ron Noland is my dad. I just can't help feeling left out in the cold." With that said Melissa continued shooting. I knew there was nothing I could say to make her feel better. She was mad and with all that's happened I'm sure she'll be that way for a long time.

It's no family secret about the differences in our fathers. Well at least it's not anymore. Long before my family started branching off in all different directions Melissa discovered documents that blew us all away. She had found papers that showed my father had adopted her and my brother, Tyrone. I was ten, Lissa was thirteen and Tyrone was turning fifteen when my mom told us the sorted details behind Melissa's find.

As it turns out, Mom was sixteen and dating Tyrone's father when she gave birth. At 18, she married a man named Derick and became pregnant with Melissa. But before Melissa was born Mom left Derick, moved to California and started dating the man who eventually became my father, Ron Noland.

When Mom and Dad married a few months after Lissa was born he adopted both children so that they could all have the same last name. The news shattered all of us. Although we noticed at a young age the differences in our appearances, we never gave it much thought. It wasn't until that night we all realized just how different we were.

Since that night, it's always been hard for Melissa not

knowing who or what she was looking at in the mirror. She has secretly told me on many occasions that she wanted to meet the man who was actually her biological father. Looking at her now I could see the hurt on her face even more so than before.

"It looks as if you're ready." Tony said while leaning on the doorframe to my room.

"Hey, and you're early." I said kissing him on the lips.

"Where are you two off to tonight?" Grandma asked as we were passing through the living room.

"Into town to get pizza, Mrs. Janie." Tony said in his southern drawl.

"Okay. Shay you be sure to call home at least once." Grandma said pointing her finger.

"Don't I always, Ma?" I said smiling. Grandma smiled back and shook her head. She trusted me and I wasn't going to do anything to mess that up. I really like the fact that she never treated me like a kid.

When we got outside my smile turned into a frown. In the country, it seemed, everybody started driving in their early teens license or not. Tony and I would both be turning fourteen in the fall and as an early birthday present, Tony and his dad had gone out today and bought a car. He wanted to be sure Tony was good on the road before school started so he could drive there.

This car, however, was not exactly what I was expecting. It's not like I thought he was getting a brand-new car but this, this was terrible. The car was a late model Ford Thunderbird with a series of dings, dents and scratches. The color appeared to be of a blue-green species. Yet if this was the best he could do to keep us from having to schedule our dates around the times when Aaron and Melissa were willing to tolerate us then I guess I shouldn't complain.

"Madam, your chariot awaits." Tony said as he dragged me to the passenger side of the car.

"This is really not funny. I thought you were buying a car?"

"I did." Tony said with a smirk.

"Okay, fine. If this is what we have to ride in then I guess I can't complain."

"Well dear, don't worry. When my dad and I are done with it you won't even remember what it looks like."

"You know that school starts in a few weeks and we can't drive to school in this." I laughed.

"Wait a minute!" Tony screamed. "Are you telling me that you're not leaving?"

Oops! I forgot that I hadn't told him and he had just been assuming that I was going back home at the end of the summer. "Well, it looks as if I'll be staying for a little while. I hope you don't mind being bothered with me a little longer."

"Are you kidding? This is going to be great." Tony said.

I'm glad he's so excited. When we first started going out, he asked if I would stay. However, I really didn't want to get into that whole girlfriend-boyfriend thing, so I told him I wasn't sure and that I really just wanted to be friends. Since that time, he hasn't asked me again to be his girlfriend. We just hung out regularly and I was very okay with that.

It was about 5:30 p.m. when we pulled in front of Porter's Pizza Parlor. Tony ordered a large mushroom and beef pizza and two sodas to go. We've been coming here nearly every Friday night since we've started hanging out together. Aaron and Melissa would drop us off here while they went to do their own thing. The pizza was almost as good as Round Tables back home.

Tonight, we decided to do something different and take our pizza to the park not far from the restaurant. Tony grabbed a blanket for the back seat and we found a nice soft spot to settle down on. We ate in silence while the evening wind blew softly around us.

"I'm going to have to stop eating like this. Between you and grandma I've probably gained twenty or thirty pounds." I said after my last slice of pizza.

"Hey, you look great to me." Tony said. "Here, come sit by me."

I slowly slid my body to his side of the blanket. Tony began to lightly touch my face and then slowly rubbed my back. I closed my eyes and relaxed as the evening breeze gently massaged my ears. Tony's hands were so soft, and I nearly dozed off. Hey…

"Tony, why do you always have to go and do things like that?" I said annoyed.

"Sorry! Don't get your panties in a bunch!"

"What! Okay, I see now that we need to have a little talk." I said resting on my bottom.

"Shay, I said I was sorry. Don't blow this out of proportion."

"Tony, look, I like you and you know it. But I've told you once and I'll tell you again. Stop trying to make passes at me because we are not now nor ever going to have sex!" I shouted.

"You want to talk about this? Fine we'll talk about it. What is the problem?"

"The problem is that I've told you before that we are not having sex not now not ever, so I'd appreciate it if you wouldn't put your hand up my shirt."

"Aeysha, I thought you liked me." Tony said.

"I do like you, but there is no way on God's green earth that I'm going to sleep with you to prove it!" I shouted. "And another thing, I don't want to keep having this conversation. So if you can't deal with that, then maybe we shouldn't hang out any more."

"Okay, okay. I know you're serious, so I will stop." He said. "For now."

I gave Tony a fatal look and asked him to drive me home. There was nothing but silence in the car on the drive back to my house. Keith Sweat's 'How Deep is Your Love' was playing on the radio. The trees were going by so fast on my side of the car that I had to break my silence to tell Tony to slow down before he killed us both. No sooner than I could get the words out of my mouth, Tony was turning onto the main street of our town.

When we pulled in front of my house I knew Tony was pissed. He didn't even bother to look my way. I wasn't going to let him leave like that so I kissed his cheek and told him to call me tomorrow. He smiled and said okay as I slide out of my side of the car. Tony didn't drive off until I was safely inside the house.

"Melissa!" I yelled from the living room.

"She's in the kitchen." Grandma said. "And stop yelling like you're the only one that lives here."

"What are you making?" I asked grandma as I stopped to see what she was doing.

"It's going to be a quilt as soon as I get enough squares."

"Oh!" I said. "Melissa."

"Ooh!" I said to Lissa when I stepped in the kitchen and saw her standing over a pot of grandma's famous collard greens with a fork.

"What are your staring at?" Melissa said.

"Ha. You know you'd better get that fork out of there and get a plate before grandma comes in here and sees you."

"I know." She laughed. "Chris stopped by to see you earlier."

"Ugh! What did he want?"

"Not much. He just said to tell you he'd call later to talk to you."

"Hey, when you're done digging around for food, do you think you'll have a minute to talk?"

Lissa took her head out of the pot long enough to say "uh huh".

We sat down in chairs on opposite sides of the table and while Melissa stuffed her face I told her what happened with Tony at the park. She did agree that Tony was wrong in his pursuit to get me to have sex with him. Then she whispered to me that she and Aaron had started having sex about two months after they met.

Well that took me completely by surprise. I had suspected that my sister had been sexually active since long before she came here. When we lived in our own house in Park Isle, California, Melissa and Tyrone would have their so-called girlfriends and boyfriends over when my mom was at work.

"Well let's put it this way, I've had enough to do with sex to last me a lifetime." I said to Lissa.

"I know your not still tripping about what happened with Paul." She said. "Shay, Mom and Paul are going to be married soon so let it go."

Lissa got up from the table and washed her plate. With her back to me she said, "All I have to say is that if you know you're not ready then don't do it and don't let him pressure you."

I could always depend on Melissa to give it to me straight. But as I sat there at the table alone in the kitchen, I tried to think of ways that would help me to let go of my past. But the more I thought about it the more I could feel Paul's hands on my body and his mouth on my breasts. Then I thought this is a good time to take a bath.

Early on a Tuesday morning after Labor Day, I found myself standing across the street from my grandmother's house waiting on a school bus. I wasn't sure if Tony was driving to school or not, but I told him last night that I was riding the bus with my friends. Grandma had gotten up early this morning and cooked a big breakfast. She made eggs, bacon, pancakes, sausage, grits and homemade biscuits. She wanted us full and ready for what was sure to be a long first day.

My first day of high school was not at all what I had expected. First of all, that bus ride should be considered a field trip. I thought we were never going to get there. I guess I should be grateful because to let my mother tell it, she'll explain to us how she had to walk ten miles to school "and that was just one way". When the bus pulled into the turnaround at school, Adrienne grabbed my arm and practically dragged me from the bus.

"Where are you taking me?" I asked. But she was too busy dodging between other students to hear me.

"Good, we made it!" She said when our bodies finally came to a stop.

"What is this line for?" I asked her.

"Breakfast. The lunchroom is inside those doors. Adrienne answered.

It must have been fifty kids in line in front of us. There was no way we'd make it through this line, eat and get to homeroom before the bell rang at eight-thirty. As Adrienne and I talked and took small steps forward slowly getting closer to the lunchroom. When we reached the counter, I could see that they were serving sausage biscuits.

I was still full from grandma's breakfast so I settled for orange juice and followed Adrienne to a table. She worked that biscuit like nobody's business, washed it down and had us in homeroom two minutes before the bell rang.

"You're good." I said when we got seated.

"You'll get used to it. Our bus is usually the last to pull in." She said smiling.

Adrienne is so funny. She was one of the first people I met when I came here a couple of summers ago. I was sitting on grandma's front porch when I saw her walking by. She stopped, introduced herself and asked if I would like to walk with her. I didn't have anything else planned at the moment, so I joined her. Now it just seems second nature for us to go walking every other day.

Well not only did I have homeroom with Adrienne; Tony was also in there with us. As the day progressed, I learned that I had all of my classes with Adrienne and three more with Tony. Was this going to be a great year or what?

Chapter 9

High School Sweethearts

"I was just calling to see what you wanted to do for your birthday." Tony said.

"I'm not sure but I will tell you this, I do not want a party and I mean it, Tony. No party!" I said into the mouthpiece of the phone.

"How about you and I having a quiet night together? I'll surprise you." He said.

"If that doesn't sound shady, I don't know what does." I laughed. I could hear that brain of his plotting as we talked on the phone and I knew he was up to no good.

"Tony, let me know what you are planning, and I'll let you know if I am willing to go." I said. "I've got to go. Call me later."

Life as I had known it with Tony changed that very first day of school. My first thought was that peer pressure was starting to get to him. Everyone knew that we were hanging out long before school started. Then he started to get a little overprotective when I started talking to other people, especially guys.

He kept wanting to sit by me in class. At lunch he would

get my tray and sit at the table with my friends and me. It was starting to drive me crazy. All the hand holding in the halls and sitting next to each other to and from school. If I decided to ride the bus with my friends, instead of driving to school, he joined us on the bus. Finally, I just had to tell him that he was smothering me. He backed off a little, but he still walks up to me when he sees me talking to another guy at school.

Anyway, I had to get off the phone with Tony because Adrienne was on her way up for our walk. Saturday's were my favorite days of the week here. After we were finished with our chores and helping grandma with the laundry, we were free to roam as long as we wanted. Adrienne and I could walk for hours without our parents sending out a search party.

Then again it would be kind of hard for anything strange to go on here unnoticed knowing that everyone in this small town knew each other. No matter what went on, news of it would spread like the wildfire. And that's good considering that a lot of the people in this town don't have a phone.

"Hey, what's going on with you and Tony? Word around school is that he likes you but…" Adrienne said as we walked our usual path.

"But what?" I said to her when her voice trailed off.

"Shay, you know that Cocoa likes Tony and has been trying to get him since before you got here."

"Okay and what does that have to do with me?" I asked.

"Shay, I'll tell you but you can't get mad. Rumor has it that you aren't really into Tony and Cocoa is using that to her advantage."

"Now Dre you know better than to listen to rumors. Let

me guess, this has to be one that Cocoa started?" I said already knowing the answer.

"I hate to say it girl, but you are giving her the ammunition to use against you."

"What is that supposed to mean Dre? You know better than anyone what goes on between me and Tony." I said getting hotter by the minute.

"Yeah I know that, but you do dis him a lot Shay." Adrienne said picking up on my anger.

"Dis him? How?"

"You talk to other guys, you barely let him get near you at school and I won't even mention that incident at lunch last week." She said.

"Oh, puleeze! Adrienne just because I am not all over Tony at every given moment like you are with Ben doesn't mean I don't like him and beside you know that Tony is not my boyfriend."

"Shay, whether you know it or not, everyone at Bridge Creek High has a boyfriend or girlfriend so I suggest you climb down off that high horse you're on and get with it. He likes you and you like him. What is the problem?"

I didn't answer because I was tired of having this conversation. I didn't understand why everyone in this small country place felt the need to be attached to somebody, anybody. I wasn't ready for that. I didn't think it was necessary to commit my life to one person when I was barely getting used to being in high school. Adrienne and I continued our walk, in silence. We stopped at the neighborhood store for junk food and Dre noticed that a crowd was forming around the baseball diamond. We took a seat on the short stack of bleachers to see who was playing.

I have always liked these get together games they played on the weekends. The teams would get out there and play and then the crowd would grow from there. Soon after the cheers would start and the game was in full swing.

After about an hour I saw Ben pull up and park on the grass to the right of us. I was hoping Dre hadn't seen him because I didn't want her to run off and leave me for him. Too late, before I could turn around to face her she was off the bench.

"Oh, look, Ben's here. I'm just going to go over and say hi then I'll be right back." She announced. "Okay, but don't disappear on me like you did the last time."

"I promise. This time I'll be back." She said with a smile.

Humph! If she doesn't come back this time she can forget calling me at least for the rest of the week. She was definitely going to be on my list of people not to talk to for a while.

I sat there on that bench for what seemed like an hour. Of course, Adrienne had disappeared. I looked around and I didn't see Ben's car anymore so I assume they went to his place, but the game was nearly over and if she has not shown her face by then I'll walk home by myself.

The home team won the game 6 to 4. I saw my aunt's boyfriend who played on the opposing team and I'm sure Yolanda was not far from him and to avoid running into her I decided to start my walk home. Adrienne had better not even think of calling me. I was not in the mood for her lame excuses.

As I approached the back of the house I could see my grandma sitting on the porch working hard at something. That woman was never without something to do. When I sat down next to her, I could see that she was shelling peas again. I wondered what she was going to cook tonight because she can really through down in a kitchen. That's probably why I've gone up a whole size in my jeans since I've been here. I got a bowl from the kitchen and started helping with the peas.

"Your friend Adrienne called. She said not to be mad and to call her back." Grandma said once I got settled. "What's that all about?"

"I won't be calling her back tonight." I replied. Then I told Grandma what she'd done for the second time. She agreed with me that I should let Adrienne stew for a day or two. I had to laugh. My Grandmother is the coolest fifty-eight-year-old I knew.

Friday has come faster than I thought it would. It was my fourteenth birthday. Tony picked me up for school as usual and after school he took me to the Mom's Kitchen restaurant in town near the school. Dre and Ben agreed to come along to help us celebrate the small and informal birthday get together.

While we were all sitting at the table stuffing our faces and talking, Tony hands me a small box wrapped in my favorite color, pink. I was a little nervous about opening it with Ben and Adrienne staring at me, but I did anyway.

Inside was a thin gold rope chain with a heart shaped pendant dangling from it. It was so beautiful. I really wasn't expecting him to buy me anything but seeing this I'm glad he did. When Ben and Tony left to pay our bill Adrienne leaned across the table to examine my new gift.

"Look at that." She said with the necklace in her hands. "That was really nice of him."

"I know. He caught me completely off guard with it." I said.

"You girls ready to go?" Ben asked as he approached the table.

"Yeah." I answered putting my hand in Tony's.

"What else are you guys doing tonight?" Adrienne asked.

"We are heading to Shay's house now. She didn't want to do anything big for her birthday." Tony said.

"Okay. Well maybe we'll see you later because we'll be hanging out at Dre's." Ben answered.

We said our good byes and headed off in opposite directions. It took us forever to get home. Tony had to stop at the store for his mom and then at the gas station. On a normal day I have to keep reminding him to slow down but not to day. He was driving slower than I'd ever seen him drive before. By the time we got to the turn that would take us into the town where we lived the sun was starting to set.

When we came to a stop in front of my house Tony was looking a little strange.

"Are you okay?" I asked.

"Not really." He said.

"Tony, we've been hanging out long enough for you to know that you can talk to me about anything." I said.

He looked up at me and said, "That's the problem. All we do is hang out."

"What are you trying to say to me? Spill it already."

"Shay, I want to be with you and I want you to be serious about me."

"Okay, and…" I said knowing full well what he was getting at.

"You are really going to make me say it, aren't you?" He

asked. "I want you to be my girlfriend."

"Is that all? Well let me think about it." I said. Before I could get the words out of my mouth Tony hung his head. I had to laugh because he was just too cute. "Oh, you know I am just kidding. I'd really like to be with you too."

"But?" He said with a hint of excitement.

"No buts. I'm serious."

Before I knew it Tony was literally in my seat and hugging me. This time I didn't bother to pull away.

Tony helped me out of the car and walked me to the door. I should have known something was wrong because the house was just too quiet. There was no noise coming from the inside like it usually was. I turned the doorknob and then all I could hear was "surprise!" My grandmother's house was packed with friends and family.

Everywhere I looked there were decorations. There was not a wall in the house that had not been decorated in some way or another. Over in the corner I spotted Dre and Ben. I'm going to have to get her alone before this night is over. I think we need to redefine our friendship because it is so plainly obvious that she knew about this party. I can't believe she was able to hold on to this without even letting a hint slip out.

Grandma let us go at it for a while. Loud music and laughter could be heard nearly half way down the street. She'd made large platters of different kinds of finger foods and a huge cake with all the trimmings. A girl is only fourteen once and this is the best one yet.

Chapter 10

Heartache

Time sure flies when you're having fun. At least that's what I've heard. I can hardly believe that it has been nearly two years since I left San Francisco. Here it is already May of 1989 and in just one short month Melissa will be making me an aunt for the second time. Personally, I think I'm a little too young to have someone calling me auntie.

It's bad enough that Tyrone has done it. I thought I would have a few more years before I had another niece or nephew. Now I'm just looking forward to seeing what sex the baby is and what he/she looks like. It's kind of exciting.

Mom said that she might try to come down for the baby's birth and when Melissa told Dad that Florine was coming he was furious. I think he wanted to come instead. He hasn't called back since that day but neither Melissa nor I are too worried about it. We know that he's dealing with a lot still.

Grandma on the other hand was the first to know that Melissa was having a baby. She told us she had a dream about fish and then she sat back and waited. One early morning about eight months ago we were on our way to the bus stop, Melissa had to run back into the house. When she came out of the bathroom Grandma was outside the door waiting. That afternoon when I got home from school Melissa and Grandma told me about the baby.

Grandma didn't get upset or yell at Melissa. She talked to her and simply said that she'd be there for as long as Melissa needed her. That was a great day. We were all happy until the time came for us to tell Mom and Dad. Mom nearly lost her mind when Melissa finally broke down and called to let her in on the fact that she was going to be a grandmother…again. Dad on the other hand simply hung up the phone. After about a month, he called her back to ask if she needed anything.

With all that drama behind us now we are just ready for this baby to get here. Over the past eight months I've watched my big sister take on more added stress than necessary. I watched her day and night, but there wasn't a thing I could do to ease her pain. Don't get me wrong, she was very happy about the baby. The agony came from people trying to tell her what she should and shouldn't do or what she could and couldn't do.

Both Aaron and Melissa were feeling the stress. At one point I thought they'd break up. However, they seem to be holding it together. He comes by to sit with her and to take her to doctor's appointments. They will graduate in June. We are not sure if Melissa will make it to graduation.

At one point, when Melissa was starting to show the principal at her school asked her if she would finish her schooling at home. They would provide the course study work she'd need to complete the twelfth grade and they'd mail her diploma to her. It seems as though the principal and a few teachers thought

Melissa would be a bad influence on the other girls.

When Grandma got wind of what they were planning to do to Melissa she got up early one morning, found a ride into town, marched right into the principal's office at Bride Creek High and gave him a good piece of her mind. As Grandma told Mr. Butler of other girls that had gotten pregnant but covered it up and of others from our town that she knew had also been pregnant. "You all will not use my granddaughter as an escape goat." Grandma told him.

After that whirlwind Mr. Butler recanted his original statement. Apparently, my grandmother knew a little about him and his family that he didn't want others to know about. I guess small town family secrets needed to stay buried and it was my grandmother who reminded him of that fact.

I am so proud of my sister. Whether she walks with her class or not, Melissa held her 3.5 GPA the entire school year. She worked so hard and it had paid off. Melissa stood up for her rights to get an education. She refused to let anyone make her out to be a black, pregnant, uneducated, dropout statistic. Good for her!

My mom is flying in next week to be a witness at the baby's birth. I am hoping she doesn't bring that thing she calls a husband. Dad and his wife called to 'wish' Melissa luck as her due date approached. I'm sure he's still not very happy with Melissa becoming a mom at such a young age, but what's done is done and I, for one, think that he should just get over it.

Six months after Mom and Paul married, Dad decided to marry some women he met at a bar. He didn't even bother to call us with news. Tyrone told us about it and since I didn't believe him I called my dad's house. When a woman answered the phone, I asked who she was and she gladly told me she was Rita Noland, Ron's wife.

"Shay, will you come out here and give me a hand?" Melissa yelled from the back yard.

"What in the world is that?" I asked once I reached the back door.

A delivery truck was backed into the yard and the driver was getting boxes from the back of the truck while Melissa signed her name on a clipboard. Three large boxes hit the ground, sending dirt in large airy swirls around Melissa and me. We stood there a moment waiting to see if he'd even volunteer to take the heavy looking boxes in for us, but it was apparent that he was not as he jumped into the drivers seat of his truck and drove off.

"Where do you think we're going with this?" I asked Lissa after trying to pick up one of the boxes and seeing that indeed it was heavy.

"I think we are going to need more help." Lissa said.

"You don't say!" I shot back.

"Okay, you're being smart now and you'd better hope someone comes along to help you."

"What? Lissa this is your stuff and if you leave me out here I will tell Grandma when she gets back. Now laugh at that." I replied.

Melissa and I stood in the back yard for only a few more minutes before my cousins showed up and were able to get the boxes in the house for us. When Melissa popped those boxes open one would have thought she'd hit a baby jackpot.

Both boxes were filled with nothing but baby stuff. Baby

clothes, diapers, powder, lotion, bottles, and bibs. Then there were bath sets with brushes, nail clippers, bath clothes and shampoo. Sets of clothes and sets of blankets. The last and largest box, held a small bassinet with a thin mattress. There was a card from my mom that said she hopes this was a good start for the baby and that she'd see us soon.

When Grandma got home later that evening Melissa and I were still searching for places in our room to put the baby's things. Grandma helped out by putting the bassinet together and after about an hour or so of struggling with that we all decided to take a break and have dinner.

"Momma, the phone is for you." I heard Yolanda say from the hallway.

As I started eating my dinner I heard a scream coming from my Grandmother that I'll never forget. By the time Melissa and I got to the hallway to see what was going on Yolanda was down on the floor with Grandma trying to pry the phone out of her hand.

Yolanda yelled into the phone at the person who had called and after a brief silence she started crying too. At the sight of this I was terrified to pick up the phone next. While Grandma and Yolanda sat on the floor balling their eyes out Melissa picked up the phone to get the scoop.

As moments passed, I prayed Melissa wouldn't lose it and I have to be next talking to the person on the phone. Melissa said a very quiet good bye then hung up. She had this shocked but scared look on her face. Tears began to stream from her eyes as she sat me down to tell me that our Uncle Luke had died earlier that morning. With Grandma and Yolanda still screaming in the hallway, I knew I wouldn't last too long there so I left to hunt down my cousins and to tell them Grandma needed all of us.

Chapter 11

Strength and Love

Today is very gloomy and it's been raining all morning. To make matters worse; it's Monday. Mom is due at the airport with Uncle Luke in an hour and Grandma's getting ready to go meet them. For the past week Yolanda and my mom have been trying to get all of the funeral arrangements together. Grandma wanted Luke buried here, so Mom and her other siblings did what they could to make it happen.

The funeral is scheduled for Saturday morning with the wake happening on Friday night. Most of my relatives that fled to San Francisco in the mid-sixties will be returning to Alabama to say good bye to Grandma's first-born child. So many have made plans to come back that we had to rent all of the rooms at the town's only Rooming House to hold them.

Grandma hasn't been doing well at all since she received that call from my mom last week. She spends most of the day sitting on the couch and every so often you'll see tears streaming down her face. Uncle Luke makes the third death of Grandma's eight children. I can't even begin to imagine how she must be feeling after losing three of her children. We've tried talking to her, but so far it's been a lost cause. She hasn't said a word in days.

Since most of the week had been spent picking family members up from the airport and bus station by late Thursday, Mom decided to have a simple old-fashioned fish fry to lighten the mood a little on an otherwise sad occasion.

As day turned into night the loud sound of voices coming from the backyard only grew. A few friends and neighbors from around town that stopped by to offer condolences stayed around to fill up on fish and beer. Grandma's sisters had actually gotten her out of the house and talking. It seemed like hours had passed as they sat back there and reminisced about Uncle Luke from the day he was born until that day he left this earth. I had begun to feel a little better about going to the wake tomorrow.

"I can't believe you people! Just like simple minded colored folk to sit around and party when somebody dies." Yolanda said standing in the doorway to the back of the house.

"Yolanda, you've had way too much to drink. Why don't you go back in the house and lay down?" I heard my Aunt Jo say.

"Hell no!" Yolanda burst out. "And Momma you shouldn't be out here with these folks as if you don't have some where to be tomorrow." She slurred.

Well, here it comes. Yolanda, as always, has had too much to drink and just has to become the life of the party. My mom was still standing over the hot cast iron pot she'd been dropping fish into watching intently. All was quiet except for Yolanda who was still fussing and cussing from the door.

When Grandma had seen just about enough, she slowly

stood and walked over to help Yolanda back in the house.

"Get your damn hands off me. You're just as bad as the rest of them out here. My brother, your first born is dead. I don't see the cause for a celebration." Yolanda yelled with tears in her eyes.

"Yolanda, we know you're hurting. We all are but don't make it worse. Let's go back inside." That was my Aunt Shelly trying to reason with her.

Grandma and Aunt Shelly stepped toward Yolanda again, but this time Yolanda started swinging her arms in an effort to keep them from taking her in. The rest of us stood to see what was going to happen and just then Yolanda swung again, but this time she hit Grandma in the head with the beer bottle she was holding. Down the stairs Grandma went landing on her back. All of us were stunned.

"Yolanda, have you lost your natural mind?" Mom screamed. "You could have killed Mudear!"

"Aw, shut up you old heifer." Yolanda slurred. "Look at 'cha. You come down here with yo' city talk, yo' city hair and yo' city attitude thinking you all that. I'm here to tell ya' California don't make you no better then anybody else."

"Yolanda, I'm not going to tell you any more to close your mouth." Mom said kneeling over Grandma. "Every time I come home you have something nasty to say."

"Go straight to hell, Florine. You don't give a shit about family. The only time you come here is when somebody dies. So you can go straight to hell. Yo' own damn kids can't stand your ass and they down here living off us."

That did it. Before Grandma could gain control of her

balance, Mom let go of her arm and lunged toward Yolanda. They fell back into the kitchen with a very loud thump. Chaos had set in. My relatives scattered in different directions. Some moved to help Grandma and most of the men jumped in the kitchen to pull Mom and Yolanda apart.

This fight took place every time Mom came to Alabama. Yolanda was about one hundred pounds heavier than my mom was, but Florine could hang with the best of them. That's for sure. Mom stayed away because of Yolanda's attitude toward her. This is mainly the reason I didn't get along with Yolanda. All the hatred and anger she felt for my mom she took out on me and Melissa. But mostly me. We did our best to ignore her and grandma always defended us but nothing seemed to matter. Yolanda had it in for us.

Grandma told Melissa and me when we first came here about the feud between her eldest and youngest daughters that has been raging for years. When my mom got pregnant with my brother some years ago, she moved to California in hopes of providing a good home life for him. She and Yolanda had been close then, but Yolanda has never accepted the fact that Mom left and never came back for her.

Of the five brothers and sisters that did migrate to California over the years, Mom was the one who'd gotten married, had the kids, the house and the job. She even had the dog. She was living the life many from her childhood could only dream of having. The sad part about her success was that she felt she had to let everyone know just how well she was doing.

My grandmother's sisters brought her into the house and placed her on the couch. There was a small cut on her head, but she seemed to be fine and flat out refused to go to the hospital. My uncles had gotten Mom and Yolanda separated, settled down and in different rooms. Knowing that the festivities were over for the night, friends and neighbors began leaving. Which was fine with me because now that it was quiet maybe I could go to bed and get some sleep.

That thought quickly vanished when I stepped into the kitchen. It was a complete mess. There was food and broken dishes everywhere. How they splattered the fruit salad on the ceiling I will never know.

"Need any help in here?" I didn't even have to look to know that voice. It was my mom's baby brother, Thomas.

"No, Uncle Thomas, I think I can handle it." I said politely.

Uncle Thomas walked over to the sink where I was standing and placed his heavy hand on my back.

"I know it's been kind of crazy around here today." He said. "But if you need to talk remember I'm always here for you."

I pulled away from him and started wiping down the stove. The sound of his voice made me want to puke and the way he stroked his hand up and down my back made my skin crawl.

"Thanks Unc, but I think I can handle it." I said.

He kissed my forehead and walked out of the kitchen. I am glad he's staying at the Rooming House with the rest of my family and even better he'll be returning to the Army right after the funeral. With the state of mind I am in right now, I'd hate to see what I'd do if he tried some of his old tricks.

After spending the better part of an hour cleaning the kitchen, I headed to my room. I found Melissa in our room sitting on the bed. I could tell she'd been crying. Melissa was a lot lighter skinned than me and when she cried not only did her eyes turn red but so did her face and hands.

"You okay?" I asked.

"Yep. I'll just be glad when this is over. It's just like black folk to act a fool when somebody dies." Melissa said.
"I know what you mean." I just had to laugh. "Do you want something to eat? I haven't seen you eat a thing all day."

"No, Shay. I'm not hungry. But what is the deal with Mom and Yolanda? Can you believe how they showed out? By the way where's Grandma?"

"Grandma was in the living room the last time I saw her. She's got a small cut on her head, but she'll be fine." I said fighting back tears thinking about all that had taken place. "I don't know what Mom was thinking. She knows how Yolanda is when she gets beer in her."

I laid down on my bed and stared into the darkness. I have never been to a wake or a funeral in my life. I could only hope my family members would remember that they are going to be in a church and act accordingly.

Saturday morning, the sun came up as if it had been there all week. Melissa and I helped Grandma put the finishing touches on the food she'd been cooking since six this morning. Grandma told Melissa that she wasn't allowed at the wake or funeral since she was so far along in her pregnancy.

I think Melissa was relieved because like me, she'd never been to one either. Grandma asked Aaron to come by and sit with Melissa while we were at the church. It was so close to her due date that Grandma didn't want her to go into labor in the house by herself.

No sooner than I got dressed did the limousine pull up in front of the house. Mom had requested four of them knowing that if anyone of the family members were left out attitudes would be all over the place. Since the church was less than three blocks I opted to walk. I just wanted to enjoy being outside and to feel the sun on my face.

Tony and Adrienne were waiting outside to walk with me to the church. Tony had been so nice to me the past couple of weeks. He didn't even question me when I told him I needed a little time to myself when I got the news of my uncle's passing.

The inside of the church was absolutely beautiful. It looks like Mom and Yolanda stopped fighting long enough to do something good. Uncle Luke had been placed in a white casket and wearing a really nice dark gray suit. I stood next to the casket looking at his face. He looked as if he was sleeping peacefully. I kissed his face and took a seat behind the rest of my family.

Candles were lit all over the church and it made a very serene feeling flow through the church. The service wasn't long at all and my family started getting a little loud with crying and wailing toward the end. Grandma didn't cry much. I guess she was just all cried out. After the pastor said his last words and the casket was rolled back to the hearse, my family piled back into the limousines headed for the cemetery and I walked back home with Tony.

Chapter 12

Birthing Baby

In the days following the funeral Melissa and I got yet another hard blow. Mom wanted us to move back to California. Actually, she told us we were coming back home at the end of the summer. She and Paul were married and they've got their lives situated so they wanted us to come be apart of it. Ha! I'm sure they do. Then Mom pulled a disappearing act and caught a flight back home.

She said she had to get back to work, but I'm sure it had more to do with the phone call from Paul saying he missed her. I think that if he missed her so bad, he should have been here to support her during a difficult time. But I'm just a teenager, what do I know? Melissa took her leaving rather hard because Mom pulled out two days before her graduation.

I can say this, it was Mom's loss because Melissa looked absolutely gorgeous in her royal blue cap and gown. Grandma and I both were in tears when Melissa's name was called, and she walked across the stage. My cousins and I were cheering so loud and for so long they had to wait for us to finish before calling the next name. I couldn't wait for the ceremony to be over so I left my seat and met Melissa on the other side of the stage just before she took her seat, to give her a great big hug. I was so proud of her. She took everything that school had thrown at her because she was pregnant and still, she came out on top.

To celebrate Melissa, Grandma cooked all of her favorite meals. A few of Melissa's friends stopped by to hang out at our house. I think having them around took her mind off the fact that Mom wasn't there. I let Melissa hang out with her friends. I was a good sister. I didn't pester her or bother her at all while they were there. After everyone had gone home, I found Melissa out back doing the one thing she loved most.

"Hey, fat girl. You shouldn't be out here playing basketball. You know if Grandma comes out here and sees you doing this, you are going to be in big trouble." I said to Lissa.
"What can I say? I love the game. Besides this baby ain't going anywhere anytime soon." Melissa said.

"Lissa, what do you think about us going home?" I asked.

"Mom didn't give us much of a choice. Aaron and I have pretty much gone our separate ways so I really have no reason to stay here. I love being here with Grandma, but now I have to think about my baby. I won't be able to work and take care of us if I stay here."

"I haven't said anything to Tony about it yet. I guess I was kind of hoping I could hide out here with Grandma until I graduate from high school." I laughed.

Melissa laughed too, but we both knew that we had no real choice in this matter because the tickets were already paid for. Mom had basically put her foot down and was not trying to hear what we had to say. I still have about a month and a half of freedom left. When I get home I'll just have to remember to keep my distance from Paul and stay as close as I can to Melissa.

"Ouch!" Melissa's shouting broke my train of thought. When I looked back towards Melissa she was bent over with her hands on her stomach.

"Lissa?" I laughed. "Are you okay?"

Melissa stood there for another minute and then let out another louder version of her first "ouch!"

"Lissa, I thought you said that the baby wasn't going any where anytime soon." I said still laughing at the site of my sister doubled over with her hands around her stomach. I pulled myself together long enough to get an arm around Melissa's waist and yell "Grandma!" as I helped her into the house.

On Father's Day, June 19th, my nephew Jonathan Sage was born. Grandma called us from the hospital early Sunday morning with the good news. But before I could get to Aaron's house to get a ride to the hospital he'd already left. I was really surprised to find that at 9:45 a.m. Tony wasn't home either. Well, I had no time to worry about the strange habits of my boyfriend I had to get to Melissa. Walking back home from Tony's house Ted and Dre spotted me and pulled over.

"What are you doing out here walking by yourself." Adrienne asked as the window on Ben's car came down.

"I just left Tony's house. My sister had her baby early this morning and I was trying to catch Aaron before he left for the hospital." I replied.

"So that's why we didn't see you in Sunday school?" She asked.

"By the way did you see Tony at church? He wasn't home

either."

"Naw!" Ben replied quickly from the driver's seat. "What time were you trying to go up to the hospital?"

"Yeah!" Dre said getting excited about the idea of getting out of the town if only for a couple of hours. "We were just going to change our clothes and then go to Mom's Kitchen for breakfast. So why don't you come to town with us and we can stop in to see your sister. You can come with us to eat."

"That sounds like a plan. Pick me up when you guys change." I said.

Ben pulled away driving in the direction of Dre's house. When I got back to the house, my cousins Shawn and Darryl were sprawled all out over the living room watching cartoons very loudly. Yolanda and her boyfriend had left for church already. Apparently, she must have thought I was going to watch these two knuckleheads all day while she was gone, but I've got other plans and she could have taken them to church with her like she does on most every other Sunday. She knew that I wanted to see Melissa today and she does this type of thing all the time just to get under my skin but I'll show her.

"You both know you're not supposed to eat all over the house and I'm not cleaning the mess you left in the kitchen. Grandma would spank your butts if she saw this."

I might as well have been talking to myself because I didn't get even the smallest response from either of them. But those are my cousins. When they get in the zone of watching television and eating, my grandmother is the only one that can make them budge from their favorite spots on the couch. I stared at them for a few seconds more and still there was no movement from either of them so, I stepped out on the front porch to wait for my ride.

My nephew was less then twenty-four hours old and absolutely adorable. I stood with my face pressed against the glass of the Infant Care Room looking down at the most amazing thing I'd ever seen. The nurse had moved Jonathan's little plastic bed right under the window so that we could get a good look at him. The sign right over his head said: "It's A Boy". My mom is really going to be mad that she missed this. Ben, Adrienne and I stood there for a few more minutes before we took off to see Melissa who was tucked away in a small Well Care Room down the hall from the Infant Care Room.

Melissa didn't look so good. She was sleeping quietly when we came in and Grandma was softly stroking her hand. Aaron was standing by the window and it looked as if he'd been up all night crying. Grandma told me the Melissa had lost a lot of blood, but the doctors said she'd be fine.

"She'll have to stay a few days but she'll be fine so, don't worry." Grandma said trying to sound cheerful. "How is everything at home?"

"When I left this morning Yolanda had already gone to church and the boys were watching TV."

"Well you go on home now. I'll tell Melissa to call you when she wakes up, okay?

"We were going to get something to eat in town before we headed back, but I won't be out too long."

"Alright." Grandma said. "Do you need any money?"

"No, Ma'am. I'll be fine."

"Don't worry about Melissa." Adrienne said when we got outside and put her arm around my shoulder giving me a really big hug. "She'll be fine. Your grandmother and Aaron will look after her."

"Yeah, I know you're right, but that's my sister." I replied trying not to cry at the memory of the sight of Melissa I had still dancing around in my head.

"Hey," Ben said. "Let's go get something to eat before I starve to death."

When we got to Mom's Kitchen it was packed as usual for a Sunday morning. Ted quickly spotted a table near the back that a waitress was cleaning off. As we walked toward the table, I heard a laugh that I knew could only be Tony's. But that couldn't be. I must really be mistaken because why would Tony be in Mom's Kitchen? Furthermore, who in the world would he be here with? All of his family was home when I stopped there this morning and Ben and Dre were with me. When we could afford it, the four of us would come here after church together. So I really had to be hearing things, right?

My heart sank to the floor when we got to the end of the aisle and in the last booth there sat Tony with Aleshia a girl from school. To make matters worse Tony was holding her hand. Now I had to be seeing things because Tony couldn't and wouldn't do this to me. He knows I'd kill him, doesn't he? Well if he doesn't know he's about to find out because if I open my eyes and they are still sitting at this table I'm going to scream.

"Okay, Aeysha, don't make matters worse. Let's just leave." I heard Dre whisper in my ear, but it was too late. I had opened my eyes and they were still sitting there. Tony had a serious dumbfounded look on his face and Aleshia was talking so fast I couldn't understand what she was saying.

"Aeysha, look, don't be upset. Tony and I are just friends." I heard Aleshia say. For the moment I was still in shock and staring totally at Tony.

"Well, aren't you going to say something Tony? What the hell is going on here?" I said as quietly as possible, which obviously wasn't quiet enough, because the couple at the table across from us had started to stare.

"Let's go outside and talk, okay." Tony answered softly as to not draw anymore attention.

"What the hell is there to talk about? You sneak out early in the morning to see another girl and now that you're busted you want to talk to me? You should have talked to me before this happened because now, you'll have to pay." I said.

I could feel my face getting hot and I knew that wasn't a good sign. I took Adrienne's advice and turned to leave before I really got loud. I could hear the footsteps of my friends marching behind me.

"What the hell made you bring them here, Ben?" I heard Tony whisper.

When I got outside to the parking lot I exploded. "Ben, you knew about this?" I screamed.

"Well kind of, Shay. But it wasn't my place to tell you." Ben answered.

"What do you mean? I'm your friend too or at least I thought I was."

"You are, Shay, but we didn't want to get between you and Tony." He said.

"We? What we? Dre please tell me you didn't know about this too. Please tell me you didn't." I begged my girl to tell me she didn't know, but I didn't know if I was prepared for her answer.

"Shay, I'm sorry." Dre said and began to cry.

I wanted to cry too. I wanted cry because I was beginning to realize that I'd wasted almost two years of my life with three people I'd grown to love and in one day I found out that they'd all stabbed me in the back. This is some kind of trend. Everyone I care about ends up hurting me worse than I had been before. The last thing I was going to do was let them see me cry. They hadn't won this game yet!

"Well, Tony I hope you are very happy with what you've done to me. You begged me to be your girlfriend and this is how you treat me?" I said.

"Now that it's out, Tony do you want to be with me or that skank?" Aleshia said.

Did she just call me a skank? Her mouth just wrote a check her butt wouldn't be able to cash. Before I could talk myself out of it, I pounced on Aleshia like an elephant to an ant. She didn't even see me coming. The adrenaline from my anger rushed through me so fast that I couldn't stop swinging and punching Aleshia. With every blow I got a small bit of satisfaction. When Ben and Tony finally got us apart Aleshia was covered in dirt and was bleeding from a cut over her right eye.

"Take me home before I really hurt somebody!" I yelled at Ben. Tony was still holding on to my arm trying to calm me down.

"Shay, don't leave it like this. We can talk about this." Tony said. That felt to me to be a true slap in the face so I slapped his as hard as I could. It must have stung him pretty good because he was still standing there shocked when I dusted myself off and got into the back seat of Ben's car. I think I've made myself clear, crystal clear, that nobody messes over Aeysha and gets away with it.

Chapter 13

Standing Up Straight

In the days that followed my very, very painful break up with Tony, I decided to surround myself with the people I love the most. Basically, I waited on Melissa and my nephew hand and foot. Wherever they went I followed. For an entire month after they were released from the hospital Grandma wouldn't allow them out of the house. Apparently, that was some sort of family tradition. They were only allowed out of the house for appointments. So, there I was warming bottles and changing diapers for Sage and then cooking and washing clothes for Melissa.

I think Melissa was really enjoying being pampered. But I let her have it because I was just so happy that she was okay. After three days in the hospital the doctors said she had gained enough strength to come home. The first week they were home was kind of a struggle. I had to fight with Aaron, his family as well as my own to spend time with my precious nephew.

Tony also stopped by that first week too. I couldn't believe he'd show his face in my house after what he'd done. When he stepped from behind Aaron once they had cleared the doorway,

I thought I would leap from my spot on the couch and scratch his eyeballs out. But I didn't, of course. I had only told my family and friends that we'd broken up. I didn't want to have to answer a bunch of questions on details so staying in my place seemed best. It was a good thing that school was out when all of this trash broke out because I know that the truth about what happened would have spread all over campus by now. I just may be able to get out of Alabama without that embarrassing thing being brought to the surface.

I didn't know how long he'd planned on being at my house with Aaron so I decide to take a walk and avoid any confrontation that I knew would take place if I had stayed. Before I could get out of the house good Tony had called after me.

"Shay, wait up!" He yelled from my grandmother's back yard.

I'd heard him call me the first couple of times, but I thought I'd pretend not to and just let him suffer a little. He reached out and touched my shoulder when he'd gotten close enough to make me stop.

"Hey, why are you avoiding me?" He asked gasping for breath.

"What?" I asked in anger.

"I'm just saying I want us to work this out some how. I hate not having you talk to me." Tony said still hunched over trying to catch his breath.

"There's nothing to work out. Don't you understand? You dissed me in front of my friends. There's no fixing that. Anyway, how could you put me down for that big faced, ugly Aleshia?" I snapped.

"It wasn't like that. I am really sorry you found out the way you did. But it all started as sort of a dare and then just got out of hand."

Tony proceeded to tell me about the bet he'd had with a couple of his idiotic friends. They had bet him that he wasn't down enough to go out with another girl because, according to them, I had Tony whipped. The last game of our high school's football season was played on a Friday night back in January and I'd decided not to go. Aleshia obviously did because that was the night Tony decided to prove to his friends that I did not have him whipped. He hooked up with her and the rest is history.

"I'm sorry!" He shouted. "I messed up and I know I did, but once it started I didn't know how to stop it. I love you and I didn't want you or Aleshia to get hurt." Before I could rethink it I'd slapped Tony right across the face.

"So you've been dating that skank for five months?" I shouted. I was beginning to feel that same adrenaline rush I had in the parking lot of that restaurant when I jumped Aleshia only a week and a half ago. It took everything I had in me to keep from kicking his natural butt.

"Shay, I want to be with you." He announced.

"No! I think you'd be better off with what you have."

"I broke it off with Aleshia that day you saw us and haven't seen or talked to her since."

"I can't believe you'd throw away our relationship on a dare. What the hell were you thinking? Proving your friends wrong was that important to you? After that first date with her you should have just told me then." I said starting to cry for the first time since the break up. I was finally starting to feel the hurt

Tony had caused.

"I didn't know how to tell you. I guess in a way I kept her around because I knew you wouldn't sleep with me." He said.

"You slept with her?" My tears had stopped dead in their tracks and the anger had returned stronger than ever. Of course, my first thought was to knock the mess out of him, but my better judgment kicked in and I figured I'd be better off cutting this conversation now before it got out of hand. "Tony," I said. "I'm going to walk this way and you go back to the house and visit with your nephew. By the time I get back there I want you gone." I looked Tony right in the eyes and added "I do not want to be with you anymore. No phone calls and no more stopping by. Okay?" I hadn't even given him a chance to reply before I turned on my heel and continued in the opposite direction of the house.

That was the very last time I'd heard or seen of Tony. I felt like my life had taken an awful turn, but I wasn't willing to let it get me down. You've been through worse, Shay.

Sage, my beautiful nephew, was gaining weight fast and in the blink of an eye, he had changed from that funky pale birth color to a honey brown. I wanted to remember everything I could about him so every chance I got I was taking his picture. "Shay, stop flashing that baby with that thing before you make him go blind." Grandma would yell at me. But he was my nephew and I couldn't help myself.

I had never heard so many folk tales in all the time I'd been with Grandma but in the days after Sage had gotten home they started pouring out of Grandma's mouth like water. We all had to wash our hands before handling the baby because he could easily get rashes. We couldn't hold him near the window or in front of the fans because the air could cause him to get colic. Grandma even flat out asked some of Melissa's friends who'd stopped by to see the baby if they were on their cycles. Grandma said a female that is not the baby's mother who was cycling could give the baby stretches if they were to hold him, whatever that means.

Melissa on the other hand seemed to have instantly become a new person. She had told me countless times, while we laid in bed at night talking, that she was going to make the best of our move back to San Francisco. She had already made plans to enroll in a community college that had a child care facility on campus. Melissa told me she was going to learn a trade and follow up by finding herself a job. After many of those late-night discussions we realized that moving back wouldn't be so bad. We would have a really hard time getting out of this small town in the future if we stayed.

She and Aaron were going to visit each other as much as they could so that he'd at least get to spend some time with his son. My plan was simple, I was going to try harder with my mom and stay the hell out of Paul's way. Besides, it was time to get back to Joann. It's amazing that we've been apart for so long and yet nothing's really changed between us. She's still my best friend. I still have every single letter she's written to me.

Chapter 14

Going Back to Cali

Melissa and I sat in the middle row of Delta flight 1508 non-stop to San Francisco International Airport. The nice blond-haired lady at the check-in counter was nice enough to put the three of us in a section of the plane where we could all sit together. However, I believe she put us towards the back of the plane just in case the baby got a little agitated during the flight. She insured that he wouldn't disturb the other passengers too bad.

We took our places in row 21 seats A, B and C. We strapped Sage's carrier into the seat between Melissa and me. I was really nervous about this trip. I don't know, maybe it was because in my heart I really didn't want to try to make this thing work with Mom and Paul. Then again it could just be the fact that this is another big change for me where I didn't know what the outcome would be. Hope for the best but prepare for the worst. Wasn't that what Grandma had always said?

The plane was roaring down the runway and I realized there was no turning back. The choice had been made whether I liked it or not. Sage did get a little rowdy when the aircraft took flight, but Grandma told us it would be from his ears popping. Before we'd left the house this morning Grandma had given Melissa some drops for his ears and some chewing gum for us to help ease the pain. That was my Grandma, always knowing what to do even before things happened. I was truly going to miss her.

I called Jo last night just to reassure her that I would definitely be on this plane today and that she'd see me real soon. I missed her a lot while I was away. The phone calls and letters didn't even come close to having her in the flesh. We'd already made plans to go school shopping as soon as I got off this plane.

When we got up this morning, Melissa and I could tell that Grandma wasn't too happy about us leaving. When Aaron pulled into the driveway to bring us to the airport, she refused to ride with us. She said that she was tired of seeing her family leave and she had no idea when she'd see us again. We said our good-byes at the back door and Yolanda took Grandma back into the house.

Melissa and I promised each other that we were not going to cry no matter what. But after seeing how hurt grandma was, we both let go of a few tears once we were inside the car. Then a few more tears on the highway and few more as we said good-bye to Aaron at the gate.

"Aeysha, you have got to stop that!" Melissa said once we were in the air. I had not even realized I had started crying again.

"Don't yell at me. You started it back at the house." I said doing my best to defend myself.

"Hey, I didn't tell you to cry." She said casually.

"So, what do you think you'll miss the most? Being with Grandma or our freedom?"

Melissa just laughed because we both knew that our days of coming and going as we pleased were going to be over soon as we set foot off this plane.

"Aaron took your leaving with the baby rather well. He barely said a word the whole drive to the airport though." I said.

"Yeah, he did better then I thought he would. But we seemed to have worked this thing out a while ago. He knows he can come out to see him whenever he wants, and I'll get back to Alabama as often as I can. The only way I can give Sage a fighting chance and to have one myself is to be someplace where I can have room to grow.

During most of the flight Melissa and I only talked in short spurts. It seemed like every time we talked and mentioned Alabama we'd start to cry all over again. It seemed like Sage was the only one not crying. After his first little outburst, he adjusted and was doing pretty well.

The flight was about six hours give or take an hour due to the time different time zones. We walked off the plane and into a very busy airport. San Francisco International was full of people scurrying about trying to make it to their respective flight gates, baggage claim or just out of the airport. After a quick stop at the bathroom, Melissa settled Sage back into his carrier, I picked up the carry-on bags and we all headed to the baggage claim area.

Mom said she would meet us outside baggage claim because she didn't want to park. One by one I grabbed our suitcases off the carousel. Melissa and I managed to pack two years of our worldly possessions and Sage's personal items into five suitcases. The guy at the airport in Meridian, Mississippi was nice enough to let us check them all without charging the extra fee for having one over the limit.

We sat outside the baggage claim silently waiting for Mom to get there. After about twenty minutes Melissa went inside to use a pay phone to call Mom at home. Who knows, maybe she got the days mixed up.

"Was she home?" I asked Melissa when she reappeared next to me.

"No. No one answered." She said looking a bit confused.

"What's the matter?" I asked.

"She had to have known we were coming in today. I called her last night to remind her of what time we would be coming in."

I could see that Melissa was getting upset. "Well, maybe she'll be here soon. She could have gotten caught in traffic or something." I said trying to shed a little light on the fact that it was cold, and we were sitting at an airport waiting for our mother.

Another thirty minutes passed before Melissa said anything else. "Okay, now this is ridiculous. I'm going to call Tyrone and see if maybe he knows where she is." With that Melissa disappeared back inside the lobby in search of another pay phone.

"Tyrone has no idea where she is, but it'll take him about forty-five minutes to get here from the East Bay. Do you still have your key to the house on your key ring?" She asked.

"Yep. I still have it, but it's down in the suitcase." I answered.

"Well, find it and I'll go back and tell Tyrone to meet us at Mom's just in case they've changed the locks."

By the time Melissa had gotten back outside I'd found the

key and was asking the attendant outside to get us a cab. When the cab pulled to the curb, Melissa was so mad that she began slinging the suitcases into the trunk of the car. The cab driver must have picked up on her vibes because he didn't say a word or pick up a suitcase.

Melissa got in the cab and told the driver the address. It had been a while since we were both in California so we wouldn't know if the driver were taking the long way or the short way. When we arrived in front of Mom's house, the meter read forty-five dollars even. Melissa paid him and we all got out of the car. The cab driver took our bags from the trunk, placing them in a neat row at the curb. I got out and tried the key in the gate. It worked! My key to the front door also worked. As the driver was pulling off, Tyrone was pulling up.

"Hey, sis!" Tyrone said to Lissa while pulling her up into one of his bear hugs. "I missed you too, Lil' Sis. Come here and let me look at you."

We stood in front of the house grinning like we'd just heard a secret and neither of us wanted to keep it to ourselves. Bobbie and the baby got out of the car to join the reunion. Ron had grown so much and from the looks of it Bobbie was doing it again. I couldn't help myself, I reached out and touch her round belly.

"What is that?" Lissa said pointing at Bobbie's protruding belly.

"It's your new nephew. So, you guys couldn't have come back at a better time." She laughed.

"Well let's go in the house and see what Mom has in the fridge to eat." Tyrone announced.

"Great idea because I'm starving." I agreed and picked up Ron to go in the house.

Tyrone brought the suitcases in while Melissa, Bobbie, the kids and I headed straight for the kitchen. This was Melissa's first time in Mom and Paul's house and she was amazed at how big it was. It was a very old Victorian house with high ceilings and hardwood floors. The amazement I felt for this house went right out the door the night I found out I'd have to share it with Paul.

Bobbie was the first to find the refrigerator and swing the doors open. "What do you guys have a taste for?" She asked peaking from around one of the open double doors.

Melissa and I just laughed.

"Hey, I am entitled to have a big appetite. I'm eating for two." She said sticking her head back into the fridge.

"It's your world, girl." I said handing Ron to Lissa so that I could go help Bobbie find something good to eat.

There was nothing in the kitchen we could all agree to eat and Lissa finally suggested Chinese. It had been a while since either of us had had any real good take out food. Where we lived in Alabama, Chinese was unheard of. Since no one else had any good suggestions and Bobbie really didn't care as long as she could eat, Chinese it was.

As I left the kitchen in search of a phone book, I could hear Sage getting worked up. I heard my brother talking to him and the noise quieted down. This was weird. Here I was sixteen years old and about to be an aunt for the third time. I walked into Paul's office for the phone book and got a cold chill. I reached down on the side of his desk, got the phone book and shot out of there like lighting.

"Girl, it took you long enough." Bobbie said when I stepped back into the kitchen. We are started laughing. I wasn't gone that long. Bobbie was just hungry.

When mom and Paul finally decided to come home, we had been through two boxes of fried rice, a box of Beef with Broccoli (my favorite), General Tso Chicken, Sweet and Sour chicken, and an order of egg rolls and were working on an order of fortune cookies. The tempo in the kitchen dropped to a near zero when Paul walked in.

"Hey girls." Mom said planting a dry kiss on Melissa's cheek and mine. Here it was nearly nine o'clock at night and she was just getting home. It wouldn't have mattered much to me any other night, but Melissa and I arrived at the airport over five hours ago and she was not there to pick us up. She hadn't even called to see if we made it and got in the house okay. Now here she comes strolling in the house as if it's all good. Melissa and I sat in silence.

"Hi, Momma." Tyrone said getting up to kiss her.

"Paul, look at my new grandbaby." She said picking up Sage.

She all but ignored Bobbie sitting in the chair nearest to her. Bobbie said not a word and continued eating from her plate. Mom and Paul played with the baby and walked back into their room but not before she warned us not to leave a single grain of rice anywhere in the kitchen.

"It looks like the party is over girls." Bobbie said looking at Tyrone. I think he got the hint quick, fast and in a hurry.

"Yeah, uh, we'll help you guys clean up and then we are out

of here. It's way past Ron's bedtime." Tyrone added.

I knew that was a crock. Ron was having a good time playing with his new cousin and spilling food all over the floor. But I could tell by the way Bobbie kind of rolled her eyes when she heard Mom come in that she was as uncomfortable being in that house as I was. As if on cue we all got up from the table and started cleaning the kitchen. I could hear Mom and Paul down the hall laughing and playing with the baby. I had to take a deep breath and count to ten. This was probably going to be the hardest thing I've had to do since birth.

Chapter 15

Getting to Know You

Last night after we cleaned the kitchen, Tyrone said good-bye to Mom and took his family home. Melissa and I were at a loss. But since it was so late it made escaping from Paul's glare that much easier. Melissa and I faked liked we were dead tired and jet lagged from the flight and got ready for bed. Mom came in our room, put Sage down on the bed and said she'd talk with us in the morning. I wanted to call Joann, but I didn't want to blow our cover so we turned the television down low and got in bed. Melissa had her nerve. She put the baby's bassinet between our beds supposedly just in case he woke up in the middle of the night looking for me. She wasn't fooling anybody. She wanted me close so I could get him in the middle of the night when he cried.

Anyhow, we spent most of the morning putting our things away and straightening up the room. Mom looked in on us a few times, but she never said much. I got tired of the quiet game and decided to call Joann.

"Hi, Mommy! How are you?" I asked as soon as Mrs. Commons answered the phone.

"Aeysha, baby, I am glad to hear your voice. Did you make it okay? Are you at your mom's house?"

"Yes." I answered. "We got in last night." I could hear Joann in the background screaming my name.

"Baby, you come by and see me soon. I'm gonna let you talk to this girl before she pees in her pants. She acts like she ain't ever got a phone call before."

"You made it!" Jo Ann said screaming into the phone. "Why didn't you call me last night?"

"Last night was pretty rough all by itself." I said. "What's going on?"

"Not much. I thought we were going to go to the mall today."

"Yeah, I know. Things are just too weird around here. From the looks of it I don't think I'll be able to get away. But I will see you at church tomorrow."

"Okay, but you know we have to get out and get back to our old routine."

"You can bet on that." I said.

"Is the number still the same?" She asked.

"Yep!"

"Cool. Then I'll call you later. Bye."

"See ya."

Just after I hung up, Mom walked back into the room and sat on my bed. "Why didn't you meet us yesterday?" I heard Melissa ask Mom.

"Paul and I had some stuff to do." Was all she'd said.

"Well, Mom the least you could have done was put it off until we got home okay." I said putting in my two cents. "What if I hadn't had my keys? We would have been standing outside all that time waiting for you."

"Aeysha, there was nothing I could do. We had a prior engagement. I couldn't just not show up."

"But you could leave you daughter's sitting at an airport for hours with no one to pick them up." My attitude was already starting to form. I had been here for less that 24 hours and already I was beginning to hate it here.

Melissa didn't say anything else. She just sat quietly while Mom ran down the rules of the house. It was pretty simple. We were to be in the house no later than 6:00 p.m., no phone calls after 8 p.m. and absolutely no company of any kind. According to mother, Paul did not want all kinds of people trampling through his house. Mom also told Melissa that she was to have a job within a week. This wasn't going to be a pleasant family experience where we all tried to get along. This was going to be a PRISON! And Paul was the warden.

"Mom, I'd really like to go to school." Lissa protested.

"And do what, Melissa? You already have a baby. I'm not going to sit in this house with him all day." Mom said.

"But we talked about this before I came here. I told you I wanted to go back to school."

"Lissa you acted like an adult when you laid down and got pregnant. You wanted to be an adult so we are going to treat you like one. You will pull your weight around here."

"Mom, what are you talking about? I mean really? I don't even have my own room but yet you want me to pull weight around here? If I work who's going to watch Sage?"

"Well, I know a few people you could use as babysitters and Paul does not want you guys scattered all over the house and messing up other rooms."

"Nah, he just wants us in the same room so he can keep an eye on us."

"Shay, please don't start that mess again. You ought to be glad Paul didn't have any objections to you coming back after that stunt you pulled."

"Whatever, Mom." I said and went on with putting my stuff away. I can't believe she's still taking up for that loser. It just makes me so mad that she has completely turned on us and what makes matters worse is that she can't even see it. I tuned out the rest of the conversation she was having with Melissa because what she was saying now was totally different from what they'd discussed before we came out here. She knows how bad Lissa wants to go to school. The girl is not dumb by far. So, she made a mistake. At least she is trying to make the most of it and not become a statistic.

When Mom finally got back on that high horse she'd rode in on and left the room I sat down on Melissa's bed next to her. I could tell she was upset. That was one thing Melissa's light brown skin could not hide. Whenever she got really mad she would get a little red in the face. That little gesture saved me a lot of times. It helped me to know when to stay the heck out of her way when she was pissed.

Between all of us, my brother, sister and I, I have been the only one who was able to basically build myself a protective shield of sorts to keep my mom words and actions away from me. But I have noticed with Melissa that she takes every negative thing my mother says like a stab in the chest. Melissa has always been a person who reacts to what others say or do. I think it will eventually catch up with her because there is no way anyone could keep taking negative blows and stay sound in their own mind. She lets way too many things affect her world and one thing I do know is that I don't want to be anywhere in the vicinity when she starts to lash out with all that bottled up anger.

For most of that first full day Melissa and I stayed in our room watching TV and talking. Sage was being such a good boy. He hardly cried much which was wonderful for me. I didn't give birth to that little boy, but think that since he's been born I've developed some real motherly qualities. I am always the first on the move when he makes so much as a whimper. Today, he was being aunt's angel.

At about four o'clock Mom stuck her head in the room to tell us that she and Paul were going out for awhile and they'd be back in a couple of hours. Paul, who was dressed in a gray three-piece suit with a dark tie, had all the audacity in the world to stick his head in and say that he hoped our first night back was a good one. When neither Melissa nor I had responded to that little statement after a few seconds had passed, Mom stepped back in to save what was left of their one sided conversation. She said goodbye for both of them then turned on her heels and disappeared.

I heard the garage door go up, then down and knew it was safe to talk. "I wonder where they're off to all dressed up." I said to the room.

"Yeah, I know what you mean." Melissa responded. "When they came in last night they were all dressed up."

"You're right. When they came last night they looked like they had been to a real expensive party."

"Well, we've been cooped up in this house all day. Why don't we go out and do something?" Lissa asked.

"Sounds like a pretty good idea, but we don't know what time they're coming back and you know yo' momma will be nice and pissed if she comes home and we are not here." I said.

"Look if she comes back and we are not here we'll just say that we went out to get something to eat and sat at the restaurant. Shay, I don't think they will be back anytime soon so don't worry."

"Hey, you know I'm not worried. I just wanted to make sure we knew what we were going to say if she got in before us."

Melissa and I got in at a quarter to eight. We both just knew Mom would be standing at the top of the stairs when we turned the key in the lock. Much to our surprise the house was still free and clear of adults and as far as we could see they had not been back at all. We'd had a great time out and seeing Mom's curled up, angry face would have only ruined it.

We took the bus up to Mission St., about an eight-minute ride from the house but a twenty-minute walk. We walked as far as we could and remembered we had to walk the same distance back so we turned around right in front of the Walgreen's pharmacy. Next to that, thank goodness, was a Burger King.

So, we wouldn't have been lying entirely when, had we'd gotten caught coming in, we told Mom that we went to get something to eat and sat at the restaurant. Sage was asleep before we got in so Melissa laid him down and then sat on the edge of my bed. She does that when she wants talk without having to ask someone to listen.

"Tell me what's eating at you so I can go to sleep. But please tell me this is not going to be a five-minute conversation on Aaron." I said sarcastically.

"Wow. I haven't heard you say that in a while." She said.

"Lissa, tell me what's wrong."

"What do you think about what Mom said about me not going to school and having to work instead?"

Shoot! I wasn't ready for this. Melissa gets all bent out of shape when she thinks people are trying to control her.

"Lissa, I think she was wrong, but how can we prove that? You should do what you think will make you happy. You came out here for a reason and that was to get yourself together so you can raise Sage. Don't let her stop you from going to school."

"Yeah, but how am I supposed to do that when she keeps saying I can't? I don't know what to do. Maybe I should just forget about school. I, at least, have a high school diploma and by the time Sage gets old enough to know anything I should be making some good money and can take care of him."

"Lissa, don't make me slap you. Do you want to go to school?" I asked frankly.

"Of course I do."

"Fine! Then that is what we will work on. You know I will help as much as I can with the baby. We will find one of those community colleges that have childcare for you to go to and then maybe a job."

"All right if you think we can do this then we have to start first thing Monday morning. I'll think of something to tell yo' momma and then we will be out."

"Cool with me. I think I still have a couple of weeks of freedom before school starts for me, so we'll just use the time wisely and make something happen."

Chapter 16

And Some Things Remain the Same

The night had given way to the morning sun before I had realized that I'd actually fallen asleep. Melissa nearly talked my ears off last night. I almost feel kind of bad that I fell asleep on her. Ha! She'll live. It was nearly 8:30 a.m. Sunday morning. Sage was moving around in his crib and his momma was still sound asleep.

My baby had to be hungry. There was no telling how long he'd been up. Goodness, he was such a good baby. He could have been screaming his head off by now, but he was quietly laying in bed waiting for someone to come to him.

How could I resist? I had to pick him up. My grandma had hipped me and Lissa to making a fresh cold bottle before we went to bed and when Sage was hungry in the middle of the night it was at room temperature for him. That was one of the best things she could have taught us.

I got back in my bed with Sage and gave him his bottle. I love the way he looked into my eyes when I was feeding him. It was like he was picking up on the kind of person I was. Sort of, like studying me. I knew right then that no matter what, he was always going to be my baby. I never really got the chance to be with Ron the way I am with Sage. So much was going on in my life when Ron was born and for much of his little life I was living in another state.

Well, hopefully, that'll all change now that Melissa and I are back in California. Both of my boys can be together now. We just have to get over to Oakland more often to spend some time with Tyrone and Bobbie.

"Hey, little man, don't you start that whining." I said to Sage when he noticed that he'd run out of milk.

"Don't be fussin' at my baby, girl." Melissa said waking up from her deep sleep.

"Girl, please this is my baby. You see who he's with." I said to her.

"Has Mommy been in here yet?" She asked.

"Nope and we've been up for a minute. Why don't you go down there and check on her." I laughed.

"You must be crazy. I'm not going down there. They must have gotten back real late last night because I didn't hear them come in. Did you?"

"No, I was too tired to listen for them. I have to go get Sage another bottle so I'll see what they're doing. Here, take the baby."

I slowly opened the door because if Mom wasn't already awake I didn't want to be the one to wake her. The house was a nineteen hundred and something Victorian, but the floors held up well to when you wanted to sneak down the hall. When I arrived at Mom's bedroom door it was wide open and the bed didn't look as if it had been slept in.

I got to the kitchen and it hadn't been touched either. That gives away the theory that they could have come in late and left early this morning. Oh, well. I really hope nothing happened to them. We wouldn't know the first friend of theirs to call to find out if they had seen or heard from Mom or Paul. I made Sage's bottle and went back to the room.

"Dang, what took you so long?" Lissa snapped when I walked back into room.

"Girl, you could have gone to get his bottle yourself. Anyhow, Mom is not down there. Their room is still clean and it doesn't look like they slept here at all last night. Do you think we should call somebody?"

"Wow, I don't know. Are you sure that they didn't just leave early or something?"

"I thought of that. But there weren't any dishes messed up and their room really doesn't look like it's been touched." I said.

"Well, the only person I can think of to call is Tyrone. Maybe he knows where they went. Go call him."

"Why do I have to go? You know his number just like I do." I snapped.

"Girl, go call him and ask him if he knows where Momma is before I get up off this bed and do something to you." Melissa said very calmly letting me know she wasn't playing.

I called Tyrone and he said that all he knew was that sometimes he'd call Mom for days and no one would answer the phone. She did tell him once that she and Paul spend a lot of time at his friend's house somewhere in the city. Now that helped a lot. I reported to Melissa what Tyrone had to say and we just sat there trying to think of what else we could do.

"Okay, obviously we are at a great disadvantage since we have not a clue who the friend is or how to reach them. So are we going to church or what?"

"Girl, aren't you in the least bit worried about Momma? How are we supposed to go to church and we don't even know if she's alright?" I asked.

"Shay, the only other thing we can do is call the police and I am not about to do that if she's just off some where with Paul's crazy butt. Besides, she's grown and can take care of herself. I'll tell you what. Let's go to church and if she's not back before we go to bed tonight, I'll call Tyrone over here and we'll call the police. Good enough?" She said.

"Well, I guess it's going to have to be. Do you know how to get to church on the bus from here?"

"You don't know?" She asked. "Shay, you did lived here before me and I know you took the bus to Joann's house from here. You were only out of the city for two years, you could not have forgotten."

"Well, I think I remember. Let's get dressed and get this adventure started early just in case we get a little lost." I laughed.

Melissa laughed too and then laid the baby down on her bed to find something for them to wear. I was worried about Mom, but I was going to see Joann today. And that was something to get excited about.

We got dressed and left the house at about 9:45 a.m. The first bus didn't take long getting to us and along the way different things started to look familiar to me, but Lissa wasn't taking any chances, as soon as we stepped on the bus she asked the driver for the correct buses to take. It turned out that we only had to take one more bus and it should let us off a block away from the church.

We arrived at church fifteen minutes before church was to start at eleven o'clock. My stomach was full of butterflies before we even got to the door. All I wanted to do was see Joann. A few people stared when we walked in, but those who remembered us came right up to us as if we'd been talking to them throughout the time we were gone.

"Can you tell me where Joann is?" I asked Denise, a girl who was about Melissa's age and was friends with her before we left.

"I think I last saw her in the kitchen with her mom." Denise answered.

"Lissa, I'll be right back, okay?" Before my sister could answer I was headed in the direction of the kitchen. The church was still the same and I recognized a lot of the people, but I just smiled and continued on my path when they spoke to me. There was no way I was stopping to speak to anyone before I found Joann.

"Joann." I whispered when I stepped into the kitchen and recognized the back side of my best friend.

"Shay!" Joann squealed. She was standing right in front of me before I could take another step. We hugged for what seemed like a lifetime. I wasn't going to be the first to let go and she apparently had the same thought. I didn't realize we were crying until Mrs. Commons came over to break us up.

"Aw, look at your faces." Mrs. Commons said laughing. "I would have thought she was leaving again they way you two are carrying on.

When It Rains It Pours

All of a sudden life began to make sense again. I was with two people I loved the most. They had endured many late nights with me. They cried with me, laughed with me and helped me through some of the hardest times in my life. These two were very important to me and now I have them back. There is no way I will ever go far from them again.

Church service could not get over fast enough for me. I wanted to race out of there and get back to Joann and Mommy's house. Not only did Joann and I have a lot to talk about, I wanted to eat some of Mommy's black-eyed peas and hot water cornbread I was certain she had made. Melissa and I parted ways after service. She wanted to get home to see if Mom and Paul had turned up in the two hours we'd been at church. I told her I'd catch the bus and be home before dark. It's not that I didn't care about my mother I just wasn't going to spend the day worrying about her and Paul. Those two have caused me enough grief over the years. I'm sure they are fine, right?

I didn't think to bring clothes to change into after church and I had gained quite a few pounds during my time spent in Alabama so I could no longer fit into Jo's clothes. I resolved to pull off my shoes, stockings and slip so that I could kick back. When we were younger we used to run around this house in just our underwear and slips on Sunday afternoons, but seeing as how we've filled out over the past couple of years I guess those days are gone for good.

Jo and I stuffed ourselves to no end. We usually began our feast by eating from Mommy's plate. Food always seemed to taste better when we ate from her plate. She used to fuss at us when we did that instead of making a plate for ourselves. But

I guess by now she was used to it and fussing usually does no good anyway. Wow! Sitting on Mommy's bed eating dinner reminded me of old times. Being in this house is so easy for me. Much of my life happened right here behind these very walls.

Mommy and Jo had really saved me from a road of disaster, but if one was to ask them about my mischievous past they'd simply say that they loved me and only did what they felt was right. I know that I'd never be able to repay them for giving their hearts and love to me. They made me feel like part of the family nearly seven years ago when I first set foot in their house. Now here we are as teenagers and absolutely nothing has changed.

I got home before dark as I'd promised Melissa. As it turns out Mom and butthead had stayed at a friend's house. When Melissa explained to Mom how worried we had been all Mom had to say was that she was an adult and there was no need for us to worry. I walked in the bedroom to find Melissa sitting in the Lazyboy holding Sage.

"Hey!" I said to her.

"Hey." Lissa said back.

"What's with you?" I asked my sister with the long face.

"I hate it here." She whispered and got up to close the door. "I'm not sure what is going on with Momma but her attitude sucks. All she thinks about is what Paul is up to. She probably wouldn't care if we ran off somewhere and never returned."

"It can't be that bad, Lissa. I guess that's how people act when they are newly married and in love."

"In love my butt. She and Daddy didn't act like that. Yeah, I'm sure they loved each other too before the divorce, but she didn't turn her back on us."

"Yeah, I guess you're right." I answered not knowing what else to say. Growing up, Mom and Lissa had always been close. I can see that not having Mom's attention is hard on her. I sure having Sage and not knowing the first thing about being a parent has a lot to do with it as well. A girl could use her mother's help.

Chapter 17

Institutional Learning

Lissa and I decided that we would get started on our plan to get her in school and find her a job. When we got up Monday morning she gave Mom some lame excuse about her going job hunting and me tagging along to tend to Sage. I found a payphone not too far from the bus stop and called Joann. She pointed us in the direction of a community college near downtown. She also said that she'd meet us out there.

The Bay Community College campus was bigger than I thought it would be and the city bus stopped right in front of it. We waited at the bus stop for about eight minutes when the next bus pulled up to the curb and off jumped Joann. Who says public transportation is good?

"You guys ready to get this thing started!" Joann yelled.

"Yep." Melissa said sounding extremely happy.

"Jo, it is way too early in the morning for anyone to be that loud." I said.

"Oh, shut up and give me that baby." She replied.

"Wow, this campus I huge. Where do we start?" Melissa

asked no one in particular.

Much to our surprise a nice-looking brother came strolling along and asked if we needed help. Melissa explained to the nice and very cute guy that she'd just moved here and that she wanted to get information about enrolling.

"That's easy." The good-looking guy said. "I am on my way to the admissions building myself so I can show you personally. I'm Stan and you are?"

"Melissa…" My sister answered with a hint of nervousness in her voice. "… and this is my sister, Aeysha, her friend Joann and that little guy is my son Sage."

"Sage? What a unique name. Well, right this way ladies." Stan said.

Stan took us directly to the admissions building as promised. Along the way he explained a little bit to Melissa about the best way to go about getting enrolled in Bay Community College. While they talked and walked a few feet ahead of us, Jo and I listened in on their conversation just in case Melissa was so smitten by brother man's good looks that she forgot something he'd told her. Yeah, right! What are little sisters for if not to spy on and listen in on her big sister's conversations? Especially, ones that included those of the opposite sex.

Once inside the admissions building, Stan directed us to the section marked 'New Student Information Center'. How easy was that? As Stan turned to leave, Melissa stood in a short line to get the information we'd traveled across town to get. Jo and I parked ourselves in chairs just outside the glassed in area where Melissa stood.

"So when are we going to get our shop on?" Jo asked.

"Hey, that is a good question. I first have to get my mom to give me some money. She's been tripping since we've been back." I said.

"How so?" Jo inquired.

"I don't know. She's just not the same. She stays out all hours of the night. She barely says two words to us and when she does she's usually fussing about something."

"Wow! Do you think it has to do with her husband?"

"I'm sure it does. Did I tell you that she quit her job because he didn't like her being away from him for so long?"

"What? That's crazy. Is he like real jealous of her?"

"I guess. Personally, I just think he's a butthead and control freak. As long as he keeps his control issues pointed in her direction and not at me I should be okay." I said to her looking around for Melissa.

"Has your mom ever said anything else to you about what he did to you?"

I have tried to years to put that incident out of my head. Once I got to Alabama I chose not to talk about it anymore. It was embarrassing and if my own mother didn't believe me, who would? When Jo asked that question it only took a second for that day to come rushing back. I just hung my head and answered with a soft "no."

Melissa resurfaced from the glass room with a smile on her face and a stack of papers in her hand. Jo and I had been talking so long that we hadn't noticed that forty-five minutes had passed.

"So, did you find what you were looking for?" I asked Lissa.

"That and then some." She answered. "Apparently, this wasn't as hard as I thought it would be. The girl at the counter explained all that I needed to do to get in, but she also suggested that I see one of the counselors to help get me started."

"Cool! So when do we see the counselor?" I asked

"Well, I have an appointment at 10:30 a.m. this morning. That means we've got about an hour to kill."

"How about we walk around the campus and see what they have going on around here." Jo suggested.

I am now very glad that Melissa made me get the stroller. I figured the carrier would be fine, but my sister wasn't having it. She'd explained that Sage wasn't as light as he used to be and carrying him around in the carrier all day would way down on our arms. Let's all take a moment to be thankful for our older sisters. Again, she was right because had we not brought the stroller along we'd be taking turns carrying my nephew all over this campus.

After passing several classroom buildings, we came upon the campus Student Center. Now, that place was nice. There was a lounge with a television that had cable, a game room, a small room with typewriters and a few word processing computers, an outside patio with tables and chairs, and a large variety of food options to choose from.

"I think I've seen enough of the campus for today. You guys want to get something to eat." Lissa asked Jo and me.

"Yep!" We both answered.

Sage was starting to get a little cranky so I am sure he was ready to eat as well.

"Spread out and get what you want. We should be able to sit, eat and make it back to admissions for my appointment." Melissa stated.

We settled down at a table on the patio. I decided on the chicken biscuit while Jo and Lissa had pancakes and eggs. I fed Sage his bottle with one hand and ate my chicken biscuit with the other. Just as we were all enjoying our breakfast, talk, dark and handsome showed up out of nowhere.

"I see you ladies are still here." Stan said standing over our table with a tray of food in his hands.

"Hi, Stan." Melissa responded. Jo and I had our mouths full so we just gave a short wave.

"Mind if I sit with you?"

"Not at all." Jo answered for Melissa moving to the chair closest to me so that Stan could have the one next to Melissa.

During our time with Stan we learned that he was in his second semester at Bay studying communications. Once he finished at Bay, he was planning to move on to San Francisco State University for his Bachelor's Degree. His ultimate goal was to become a radio disc jockey. I could definitely see him doing a job like that. He seemed like a good people person. Jo and I excused ourselves from the table to throw away our trash. Melissa got up a few minutes after we did. We all waved good-bye to Stan who was still sitting at the table and had pulled out a book to start studying. We made it back to admissions with a few minutes to spare before Melissa's appointment.

"Hey, did he give you his number?" Jo asked Melissa once we were sitting down.

"Well, if you to busy bodies must know, yes, he did." Melissa answered.

Jo and I let out a little squeal while Melissa just smiled. I was happy for her. He seemed like a nice enough guy and

Lissa hasn't really gone out since she and Aaron broke up. Stan already knows she has a baby so he must be cool with that to offer her his number.

"That was a good move getting his number." I said. "The way

Mom's been acting it would probably be best that he didn't call the house."

"You are right about that." Melissa responded with a laugh.

"Melissa Noland." That was the lady over by the glass room calling Melissa in to see the counselor.

When Melissa and I had made it back to the house, Mom and Paul were gone. No note as to where they'd gone or when they'd be back. This, of course, was no surprise. Melissa and I called our favorite Chinese restaurant on the corner down the block from the house to place the usual order. After about ten minutes I left the house to go make the pick up.

Melissa and I sat on our beds with the television on eating our food. It was getting late and we wanted to be fed and ready for bed before Mom and Paul got home, that is if they even bothered to come home. Melissa talked about all that had happened at Bay Community today. She was very excited about the possibility of going to college. The counselor had informed her that all she really needed to be enrolled was her high school transcripts and a completed application with the twenty-dollar processing fee.

With Melissa being a California resident tuition fees weren't going to be too expensive. The counselor explained all of her financial options from scholarships to student loans. With Melissa being a single parent, she could qualify for a couple of grants. The counselor gave Melissa a form to apply for the Work-Study Program offered there. This will allow Melissa to work right there on campus. What's even better, there is a child care center on-site.

She also gave Melissa a catalog with a listing of all of the majors offered there. Now, she just needed to decide what she wanted to spend the rest of her life doing and off she goes. Well, it seems as if our little plan to get Melissa in college just might happen. I am so excited for her. She is a very smart girl and once she puts her mind to something, she will definitely go after it wholeheartedly.

"So, what did you think of Stan?" I asked once Melissa stopped talking about Bay Community.

"Girl, don't you ever think about anything other that boys?"

"Hey, I am a sixteen-year-old female. What do you expect?" I laughed.

"I think he's nice. I figured I'd make him sweat a couple of days and then give him a call. I might even let him take me out on a date."

"Hey, a date would be great. Hope you can find a good babysitter."

"Yeah, right, how could I ever replace the best babysitter ever...you."

I just laughed. I knew when my sister got pregnant that I would be the designated babysitter. But that's okay. Sage is such a good little boy. With the television still on and the lamp still shining Melissa and I dozed off to sleep. After what seemed like only a few minutes of sleep I heard Mom and Paul arguing as they came into the house.

"Hey, Shay, are you sleeping?" I heard Melissa whisper.

"I was."

"Do you hear that?" She asked.

"Yeah, that's just Mom and Paul arguing." I answered. The voices had faded some since I'd first heard them. I guess they'd made it into there room and had the door closed.

"Did you hear that?" Melissa said just a little bit louder.

"Yeah, it sounded like something fell." Before I could finish my sentence, the sound came again just slightly louder than the first. With that Melissa and I were both up and at the bedroom door. The voices got louder followed by more banging. The hallway was dark when we cracked the door, but we knew Mom and Paul were in their room because their door was slightly ajar with the light on.

"I'm going down there." Melissa said and headed down the long hallway. Just then Mom let out a painful yell followed by another bang. Melissa sped up with me following close behind.

"What the hell!?" Was all I heard Melissa say when she made it to their bedroom door.

I could not believe my eyes. The room was a wreck. Paul had Mom down on the bed slapping her in the face. Melissa had jumped right in the middle pushing Paul into the dresser. Mom was still holding onto her face and rolling around on the bed when Paul charged after Melissa. I was in shock, but I wasn't too stiff to run to the office and to pick up the phone. I dialed Tyrone's number with the quickness.

"Ty, Paul jumped on Mom and Melissa. He's lost his mind." I yelled into the phone.

"What?! Shay, what's going on over there? What is that

noise?" Tyrone yelled back.

"Paul is fighting with Mom and Melissa. He beat up on Mom. Melissa jumped in to stop him and now they're all fighting!"

"Call the police and I am on my way." With that Tyrone hung up the phone.

My next call was to the police. I was in tears as I listened to my mom and Melissa yelling and screaming as they tried to fight Paul. I have no idea what set him off, but he was mad and didn't seem to be slowing down.

"Hello. Police? My stepfather is hurting my mom and my sister. Please, come and help us!!" I said to the lady on the phone.

"Sweetheart, what is your address?" The lady said calmly. "Honey, try to take a deep breath and think. What is your address?"

Between the tears and the fast breathing I spewed out my address. I held on to the phone and listened to the lady on the phone as she tried her best to keep me calm. All around me I could hear things crashing and breaking in the room where Mom and Melissa were with Paul. I tried to keep my mind away from the thought of him hurting them badly.

"Sweetheart, can you see what is happening?" The lady asked breaking into my thoughts.

"No, I'm down the hall. I can't see them, but I can hear them screaming." I was sobbing big time at this point.

After what seemed like hours the doorbell rang. There was a gate across our front entry way before you could get to the door. So, I told the lady that I had to go and let the police in. I stepped out into the hallway and felt an instant headache. Paul had grabbed me by the hair as I headed to the door. I let out a scream just as the doorbell rang again. I could hear the police yelling out and pounding on the gate as Paul slammed me against the wall.

As I began to slide down the wall I could hear headed down the stairs. Next, I heard him talking to the police. I heard them asking him to open the gate and Paul fumbling with his words to explain that everything was okay. I heard someone scream, but I didn't know who. It came from the room where Mom and Melissa were. I realized at that time that I had not heard a sound from that room in quite some time.

Everything was in a fog. I heard voices all around me but had a hard time focusing on anyone of them in particular. There was a light shining in my eyes and a man's voice asking me if I could see him and if I knew where I was. I couldn't focus my eyes very well, but I knew where I was. I didn't exactly know what had happened to me to cause me to be on the floor. I could also recognize Tyrone's voice though. He was yelling something and then there was another voice telling him to try to stay calm.

"Ty?" was the last thing I heard from my mouth before I woke up in the hospital bed. When I opened my eyes I saw Bobbie sitting in a chair in the corner of the room. She looked up from her magazine when I had stared long enough for her to feel it.

"How are you, Champ?" Bobbie asked moving closer to me.

"I guess I am okay. My head is pounding like a bomb has gone off inside my brain"

"Well, not to worry. The doctor says that you will be fine."

She replied with a weak smile.

"Where is everyone else?" I asked softly.

" Florine and Melissa went down to the cafeteria to get something to eat and the boys are with my sister."

"Where's Tyrone and how long have I been here anyway?" I asked.

"You have always been one to ask a lot of questions, haven't you?" She tried to laugh it off, but I knew she was choosing her words carefully.

"Bobbie, what are you not telling me? What happened?"

"Okay, I guess you're a big girl and I'm not one to lie. You have been here a day and a half. When Paul slammed you into the wall you got a concussion and the doctors figured that caused the slight comatose state you were in. Ty is in jail. The officers said that he assaulted one of them when they tried to keep him from beating down Paul."

"Go, big brother." I cheered. "Sorry." I replied when I realized that this was not good news to Bobbie.

"Well, don't go cheering just yet, little sister. Paul was arrested that night too but, you know Florine, she went down and got him out."

"Girl, Bobbie, please tell me that you are lying. She went and got Paul and left Ty there?"

"Well, she said that she didn't have money to get them both out at the time so now we are supposedly trying to get up the money now."

"Bobbie, I know you were ready to spit bullets!" I shouted.

"Shay, calm down! I don't want your mother coming back in here saying I upset you and definitely don't let her know that

I filled you in on what's been going on."

With that being said I shut up but was still fuming. My mother must be out of her mind. She will bail out the fool who put me in this bed but leave my brother in jail knowing full well that he had every right to want to beat Paul's natural behind. I kept my silence when Mom and Melissa came back into the room. Talk about having a splitting headache.

Chapter 18

Trials of Love

Weeks following my release from the hospital were pretty quiet on the home front. Mom said she'd forgiven Paul for what he'd done and we were no longer going to speak about the "incident". I, for one, had not and would not forgive that mad man for anything. He has done so many terrible things, not only to me, but to the rest of my family. Melissa and I talked about the "incident" the first chance we got after Mom and Paul had left the house one afternoon. Melissa cried as she told me what happened in their room that night. I cried right along with her because I could simply feel my sister's pain and frustration.

Paul was so enraged that she had interrupted his beating on our mother that he grabbed Melissa and started hitting on her. When my mother collected herself, she jumped on Paul trying to get him off Melissa. Melissa picked up what ever she could to throw at or hit him with. She and Mom both had noticeable bruising and scars about the face, neck, arms and hands.

Neither of us could understand why Mom stayed. I guess that's one of those lessons we'll figure out when we are grown and on our own. Melissa and I stayed together at all times. Whether we were in the house or out, we were together. We feared for each others safety. The more we stayed in that house the worse things seemed to get and more distance seemed to grow between my mother and us.

A few days after I returned home from the hospital Paul came into our room to apologize. Mom was right there behind him, supporting and agreeing with his every word. "We must put this past us" he said. "As a family, we have to stand by each other in good and bad times." He continued rambling on like that for nearly thirty minutes. When it was all over, he walked over to me, took my hand, gazed into my eyes and said that he was truly sorry for hurting me. Mom must have been eating up that junk he was spewing because she stood at the doorway in tears. She really seemed very moved.

I was not buying that bag of bologna he was selling, and neither was Melissa. I pulled my hand away and laid down on my bed hoping he could take the hint. How could a person claim to love another and yet continue to hurt the one they supposedly love? I simply do not understand.

I hadn't seen Ty since the night of the "incident". Bobbie did call to say that they'd gotten together enough money to get him out. Still, we haven't heard from him. I am sure he is very upset with Mom. Tyrone had spent nearly a week in the downtown lock up waiting for someone to come and get him, my poor brother. All he was trying to do was protect us. Somehow, Paul had convinced Mom that Tyrone deserved to be in jail because he'd come into their home and butting into a family disagreement. At this point in my life I knew that nothing in my family would be the same again.

Mom and Paul stepped out for the evening to "talk things over." I decided to call my brother. I wanted to know how he was and what he was thinking. I got no answer.

"Were you able to get him?" Lissa asked when I returned the phone to its cradle.

"Nope, just got the machine." I answered.

"He probably won't call back. I'm sure he is plenty pissed." She said.

"Yeah I know, but at least he'll know that I am thinking about him."

"So, what do you want to do about dinner?" Melissa asked.

"Lissa, I'm not so hungry right now."

"Aeysha, you've got to eat. Don't let what Mom and Paul do worry you to death. Unfortunately, they are the adults and we have to deal with them for the time being. But I promise you, I won't let anything happen to you again." Melissa said starting to cry.

"Hey, what's with the waterworks?" I asked in a bit of a shock seeing my sister crying.

"I just wish that there was more I could have done to help you that's all."

"Melissa," I yelled! "You did all that you could short of killing the man to help me and Mom for that matter. Don't blame yourself. It is not your fault."

I walked over to my sister's bed and sat down to cry with her. We just held on to each other and cried. I know she felt just as trapped as I did to be in this house. There was no way out. It wasn't like we could just up and run away because we had Sage to look after. Going back to Alabama was out of the question because that would be the first place Mom would look for us. I also know that none of our relatives would be willing to hide us from her. Tyrone probably would, but his place is too small and we'd just be bringing more trouble for him and Bobbie. Melissa and I were trapped. All we could do now is rely on each other.

"How much money do you have?" I asked trying to take Lissa's mind off of our problems.

"I think I have about fifty bucks left, why?"

"Pizza, that's why! We haven't had pizza in awhile. Let's go to Round Tables." I suggested.

"That's the best idea you've had all year." Melissa joked.

I grabbed my jacket and ran to the kitchen to get Sage a couple of bottles. It was still early so we could get a large pizza and have some left over for later.

"Hey, I know you don't think I'm paying for pizza all by myself. How much do you have and don't lie?" Melissa asked as we were on our way out the door.

"I only have a twenty left. I am hoping Dad will be mailing some more money soon." I laughed.

"You and me both." Melissa said.

Just like clock work the Number 14 bus going to Mission Street pulled up to the curb ten minutes after we got to the stop. Our twelve-minute ride was over much sooner than we expected. We made the short walk from the bus stop to the Round Tables Pizza restaurant in the middle of the next block. We ordered a large pizza with half pepperoni and half mushroom and sausage and a pitcher of Coke.

No matter how hard she tried, there was no way Melissa would ever get me to eat mushrooms. It is always nice eating at

Round Tables. They bring the pizza out to you piping hot with the cheese still bubbling. They also had a pretty nice game room with a Pac-Man and Ms. Pac-Man arcade machines. Lissa is great at both. She could drop in a quarter and play for an hour. I never lasted that long. I think ten minutes is my max.

It was nearly dark when Melissa and I finally got back to the house. We hadn't expected to see Mom or Paul when we got there and were excited to find that they didn't disappoint us. As soon as I stuck my key in the door the phone started ringing. I swung open the door and took two stairs at a time until I reached the top, then made the left turn to our bedroom. I was out of breath, but I answered the phone on the third ring.

"Melissa, it's Ty. Come get the phone. Bobbie's going into labor." I squealed from the top of the stairs.

"Well, don't just stand there looking like a goofball, come help me."

I went downstairs to trade places with my sister while she ran upstairs to get the phone. I didn't even bother to take Sage out of his stroller. I just pulled him up the stairs in it backwards. Melissa hated when I did that, but tonight she'd just have to understand. Melissa said a few more "uh huh's" and a couple of "okay's" then hung up the phone.

"I'm gonna be an aunt! I'm gonna be an aunt!" I sang.

"Will you stop that? I hated it when you did that after you found out about Sage and I hate it even more now." Melissa said popping me upside the head.

"So what happened? What did he say?" I asked.

"He said that Bobbie was fine and she just started having pains. He was going to take Ronnie to the little old lady next door and then take Bobbie to the hospital. I told him we'd come stay the night and pick up Ronnie."

"Well, how the heck are we supposed to tell Mom all that when we don't know where she is or how to get in touch with her."

"She and Paul probably won't be back tonight anyhow so we will just leave her a note."

I looked at Melissa kind of funny because she knows how Mom is about us being out after dark. Melissa just threw her hands up knowing full well what I was thinking then turned toward the room to pack an overnight bag. I quickly joined her figuring that I'd be better off going with her then being at home when Mom and Paul decided to show up. Melissa left a note, we locked up and left.

Melissa and I got up the next morning and took little Ron to the hospital to see his new baby brother, Austin Michael. My new nephew is absolutely gorgeous. He has a full head of hair, big round eyes and a cute little nose. Wow, I couldn't believe it. Once again, I became an aunt. Three little boys and they are all mine. I never thought being an aunt would be so great.

Bobbie looked exhausted when we made it to her room. Tyrone said that she'd be fine once she ate something. She had been up most of the night holding the baby. Tyrone and Bobbie are great parents, young, but great. Ron ran into the room right into Tyrone's arms.

"Bobbie, Austin looks great!" I squealed. "How are you feeling?"

"I am doing fine. I want them to bring my baby back, but the nurse said that I had to eat first." Bobbie replied with a sadness in her eyes.

"Well, do what the nurse said and you can have your baby!" Lissa said coming up behind me to kiss Bobbie hello.

Tyrone took Sage and Ron to the children's play area so Lissa and I could fuss over Bobbie. Bobbie told us all about her laboring and birthing process and maybe just a little more than I needed to know. I loved my nephews, this is true, but a mental picture of their birth is something I don't need. Melissa spoon fed Bobbie her lunch while I flipped through the channels for something to watch.

"Ty, you should get home and get some sleep. We'll keep Ronnie here with us." Melissa said to our big brother.

"I'm alright, Sis. I caught some sleep on that flip out thing over there that they call a bed." Tyrone said.

We all laughed at the thought of Tyrone's 6 foot 2 body stretched out on that little bed/chair thing in the corner of the room. The nurse came in with Austin just as promised and Bobbie's face lit up. Tyrone and Ron climbed up on the bed to get a closer look at the baby. No sooner then they got settled on the bed that Melissa broke out the camera. One thing is for sure, our family loves to capture moments like this on film.

The door to Bobbie's room swung open and in walked Mom and Paul with big smiles on their faces. As they came in the room fell silent. Mom walked over to Bobbie's bed to see Austin while Paul stood dumbfounded in the middle of the room. Still no one said a word. I guess Melissa could sense Tyrone's anger burning because she walked over to him, whispered something in his ear, with that Tyrone kissed Bobbie on the cheek and left the room.

Chapter 19

What Was I Thinking?

A couple of days ago are probably when I truly realized that something was a little off about my family. Actually, it was the very day Mom and Paul walked into Bobbie's hospital room as if nothing in the world had happened days earlier to make Tyrone stiffen up at the sight of Paul. I am thankful that Melissa saw enough in Tyrone's expression to get him out of that room quick. Paul didn't say much that day and neither did Mom. She held the baby for a few seconds, made nice talk with Bobbie, kissed Ronnie and said good bye.

I was shocked she didn't say anything about Lissa and me not being home and leaving that stupid note. She didn't even bother to ask us when we'd be home. There was simply something very strange happening to Mom and I didn't quite know what it was. However, I did know this; what ever it was I could bet my life that Paul had something to do with it.

Melissa and I took advantage of Mom's weak state and stayed another night at Tyrone's with Ronnie. Bobbie was to be released from the hospital the following day and Tyrone wanted to stay with her at the hospital. When we arrived back Ty's place

Melissa started to feel guilty so she called Mom and like usual no one answered. Melissa left a message letting her know that we wouldn't be home that night either.

When Melissa and I returned home, the house was empty. It was still early in the afternoon so we decided to stay in and enjoy the quiet around us. I flipped on the TV to see if there was anything good we could watch. Sage was sleeping peacefully in the middle of my bed.

"Hey, I am going in the den to use the phone. Let me know if you hear them coming." Melissa said once she got her coat off.

"No problem. Who are you calling anyway?"

"Now, that is none of your business Miss Thang."

While Melissa ran off to make her secret phone call, I curled up on the bed next to Sage. Flipping through the channels I found nothing interesting, so I stopped on the music video channel. I realized in that moment that school was starting in less than a week and a half. With all the stuff going on in my family I'd hadn't had a chance to go school shopping, not to mention that I hadn't talked to Joann in a while. I really need to talk to her and let her know all that's been happening to me. She has no idea that I was even in the hospital let alone that I had a slight concussion thanks to my wonderful step-father.

Mom and I really haven't been talking much this summer, so I had no idea if she'd enrolled me at Joann's school like I'd asked her to. Well, I hope she is in a good mood whenever she gets home so that we can get this stuff settled.

"Are you sleeping?!" Melissa shouted as she came back into the room from her phone call.

"No and stop yelling before you wake the baby you, old

crazy girl." I shot back with a little attitude. Sage hadn't been sleeping that long, but I wanted him to sleep a little longer.

"Who you calling crazy? Don't make me have to beat you down."

"Ha! Not likely. So, who was on the phone?" I asked again.

"If you must know I called Ty to let him know we were home and then I called Stan."

"Oh, so now we get to the good stuff." I said sitting up on my bed.

"No, there is no good stuff. We just talked about school and when I would be starting."

"Girl, forget all that. When are you guys going out?" I asked a little more interested now.

"Shay, what is with these twenty questions?"

"Lissa, come off it. When are you going to go out with him?"

"It's not that simple. I have a baby just in case you didn't notice and you know Mom would have a fit it I started talking about going out somewhere."

"All that is true, big sister, but I can cover the baby situation and who says Mom has to know that you are going out? She is here so little that there is plenty that we could do that she'd never find out about." I responded coldly.

"You are serious, aren't you?" Lissa asked suspiciously.

"Ain't nothing to it, girlfriend. If you want to go out with Stan we can make it happen and I can guarantee we won't get busted." I had to laugh at myself. I didn't realize how devious I could actually be when pushed to my limit. "So, are we gonna do this or what?"

"Well, he did ask if I could go out to a movie or something

on Friday night, but I told him I had plans." Lissa responded.

"Well, go tell him that your plans have changed and find out exactly what he wants to do so we can get a good idea of how much time we'll have to account for with Mom."

With that little bit of encouragement Melissa ran off to the phone again. I sat on the bed going over in my mind just how we'd get away from Mom long enough for Melissa to have a date with Stan. This shouldn't be that hard since Mom and Paul usually spend every weekend out of the house anyway. With our luck this will be the weekend they decide to stay at home which means Melissa and I will just have to be a little more creative in our plan.

Besides all that, Melissa is a grown woman. She should be able to go out without our mother tripping out. Probably the only way either of us will get out of this prison is to meet someone and run off. I can only hope someday Mom will realize how miserable she's making us and leave that fool she calls a husband. Even if Lissa and I were to go to live with Dad things more than likely wouldn't be any better. He's always working and I have never met my step-mother so I can only imagine what she's like.

"It's all set! We are just going out to have an early dinner because Stan has to go in to work late Friday night." Melissa said snapping me out of my thoughts.

"Cool! Is he planning on picking you up or are you meeting him?" I asked.

"He is picking me up."

"Where does he live?"

"Somewhere off Third St."

"Oh, my gosh this is too easy."

"Okay, girl, don't go underestimating your momma."

"Lissa, he can pick you up from Mommy's!" I said extremely excited that this was going to be easier than I thought.

"What?" My sister asked with a seriously confused look on her face.

"Lissa, it's very simple. We will go over to Mommy's early on Friday, spend the day over there and he can pick you up from there. You all can have dinner and we can hop the bus back home." I explained slowly. "Jo and I have to go school shopping anyway so we can tell Mom that that's what we are doing. You know she never checks on me when I am over there."

A smile came over Melissa's face after she realized what I was saying. Mommy would never rat us out and Jo was always down for a good sneak mission. Don't get me wrong if Mommy thought Melissa and I were up to no good she wouldn't help us or condone it. However, she's been around a long time and she knows how much my mom has changed. Some of the stuff Mom does simple does not make sense to anyone but her.

Mom and Paul walked in the door at about 9:00 p.m. which was early for those two. I figured I'd let her get settled in before I went in to ask her about school and remind her that it was going to start soon. She peeked her head in the door of our bedroom to make sure we were where we were supposed to be. She didn't even bother to ask us what we'd done all day or if we'd eaten dinner. She said a simple and dry 'hello' and then she was gone.

I figured thirty minutes was enough for her to get herself together. I took a deep breath, gave Melissa one last look and at exactly 9:30 p.m. I walked out of our room and down the hall to Mom's room. I didn't dare walk in even though the door was open. Paul was standing near his dresser talking about something my mom had done that was "just so stupid." When he looked up and saw me standing there in the door way hatred filled his already burning eyes.

"What can I do for you?!" He snapped.

Mom looked up from her lap and immediately got up from her spot on the bed. She walked me down the hall and into the kitchen before she said a word.

"What's wrong with you coming into the room like that?" She said.

"I wasn't in the room. I was standing in the hallway." I smarted back to her.

"Shay, I don't have time for your mess tonight. What do you want?" She asked taking a seat at the kitchen table.

"Well, I just wanted to ask you if you were able to get me registered at Stewart High like I'd asked. Not to mention school is starting soon and I have yet to go shopping."

"Honey, I thought it would be best if you went to Ignacio Christian Academy so that is where you are going. Remind me to give you some money on Friday and you can go shopping with Joann. I know you'd both like that. But you'll only need to get school supplies because you'll have to wear a uniform at ICA."

Okay, I picked on the Friday thing. Mine and Melissa's plan was definitely coming together much better than we could have hoped for. But don't think I missed that whole Christian School thing.

"Mom, you can't be serious! You what me to go to that

Christian school up the street? What about Jo? You know we've been planning to go to high school together practically since the day we met."

"Shay, you went to a Christian school when we lived in Oakland. What's the matter with that?"

"Mom, did you know that that school is an all girls' school? Forget all that, what am I supposed to tell Jo?"

"Shay, trust me it is easier for you to go there and get right home after school rather than taking a bus to Joann's side of town to go to school. Besides, an all girls school might keep you from making the same mistake your sister did." She said.

"Is that what this is about? What Melissa did is her own drama. That doesn't mean I'm going to do the same thing." I was mad that Mom could think so little of me.

"Shay, you are giving me a headache." Now Mom was starting to get mad.

"What is up with you, Mom? Why are we even here? I'm not happy. Melissa's not happy and most of all you're not happy." That just came from nowhere, but Mom was tripping and nothing else anyone said seemed to matter to her.

"Lower your voice! Who are you to tell me that I am not happy? You're only a teenager what can you possible know about happiness?" Mom said with much attitude. "Shay, baby, there is a lot that you just don't understand. I don't have a job anymore. Where can we go? Where would we live and how can I support us on nothing."

"Mom, anything has got to be better than this," I whispered.

Before Mom could respond Paul appeared in the doorway. "I'm going to bed" he said and walked away. Mom stood, said she loved me and followed Paul to bed. I sat there at the table still stunned by what Mom had just said. She was miserable and refused to see it. I may only be young but I do know this, in all the years my parents had been married I'd never witnessed my father so much as raise a hand to my mother in play. He would have never hit her. He barely liked spanking us.

 And Christian school? Uniforms? What was I supposed to do there with a bunch of girls? How was I going to explain this to Jo? High school was going to be our time together before we got separated again during our college years. I know there would be no way to change Mom's mind. This woman is dead set on ruining my life.

By the time Friday began to make its mark on the world, Melissa and I had worked the perfect plan. Although, with Mom being so unattached these days she was making it too easy for Melissa and I to pull it off. The three of us Melissa, Jo and I, decided that it would be best to start our shopping late in the afternoon that way if Stan and Melissa needed more time it wouldn't be hard to come up with since the mall didn't close until 9:00 p.m. Best of all Mommy said she'd keep the baby while we went shopping. Is that not the best?

We explained to Mommy what we were up to and why Stan needed to pick Melissa up at her house instead of ours. There was no need to lie to her since we weren't actually doing anything wrong. Melissa was nearly nineteen years old and she should go out on dates every once in awhile. Mom is simply being ridiculous with all of her rules and regulations at the prison. Sometimes a person has just got to break free!

Melissa and I headed for the bus stop at about 1:00 p.m. It would take us nearly thirty minutes or so to get to Jo's and Stan was going to pick us all up at Mommy's around two. He will drop me and Jo off at the mall while he and Melissa went off to have their date. When I told Mom that Melissa was going to come with Jo and me she said it was a good idea. Not only would Lissa be able to keep an eye on me, but she can apply for work at some of the stores in the mall.

"Are you nervous?" I asked Lissa once we were settled on the bus.

"Not really. Mom and Paul will be leaving the house soon and she probably won't give us another thought.

"That, my sister, is the truth." I said. "What about your date? Are you nervous?"

"I will be if you keep talking about it." She said with a smile.

No, I didn't feel bad at all that we were pulling a sneak job on Mom. Just the look on my sister's face at that moment confirmed it for me. Melissa smiled a genuinely happy smile. That is one that I hadn't seen in a while. Stan seemed like a cool guy, however, if he hurt my sister, I would not hesitate to call in reinforcements from the ghetto side of my family to set him straight.

Chapter 20

The Morning After

Ignacio Christian Academy for Girls was truly not the place I had envisioned spending the rest of my high school years. Jo took the news of us not going to high school together very hard. "Has your mom really lost her mind?" She asked. The more I thought about it the more I was convinced that Mom had lost it. High school is a defining moment in a young girl's life and she'd totally kicked mine to the dogs.

ICA, I quickly learned, was only about two percent Black. The school took up half a city block and housed less than 500 students. After about a day or two I felt a little bit more at ease. I still wanted to be with Jo, but ICA wasn't feeling too bad. The girls and my teachers were super nice. Actually, I thought they might have all been on drugs because they were so happy all the time. I'd never seen anything like it.

Sherry, one of the girls I met on the first day, helped me to make the most of my uniform since it would be the thing I wore the most over the next couple of years. She taught me how to roll my skirt just right, high enough for me to look cute but not so high that the Sister's would have to send me to the office. It wasn't as hard as I thought it would be to fit in. So, I'd have to wear a plaid skirt, white shirt and burgundy cardigan every day. I guess I could live with that.

As school was beginning for me, life at home seemed to have calmed some. Melissa had a week to go before school was to start for her. We hadn't quite worked out a plan on how to break the news to Mom yet. Bobbie suggested that we don't tell her at all. "Tell her you got a job at some office and then leave every morning like you were going to work all day." Bobbie said. It could work, for awhile anyway. We'd just have to hide Melissa's books and she'd have to be creative about studying, but it could work.

Unfortunately, we would never get the chance to see if our plan would work. I came home on Thursday afternoon of my second week of school to find that all hell had broken loose at the house. Melissa was crying and so upset. Paul and Mom were nowhere to be found.

"What is the deal? What's going on?" I asked as I walked into our room and saw Melissa one her bed with her head in her hands. I thought the news of Mom asking Dad for a divorce was the shock of my life. Nothing could have prepared me for what was going to come out of my sister's mouth that day.

"She left." Lissa said.

"Girl, what are you taking about? What has you so upset?" I asked starting to cry myself.

"Mom! She's gone! She left!" Melissa said.

"Stop crying, Lissa and speak in complete sentences." I yelled at her.

Melissa took a moment to gather her thoughts and calm

down. Sage was on the floor playing with his toys oblivious to what was going on. As Melissa began to talk my body went cold. My mother had not come home the night before but that wasn't unusual. When she did finally arrive after I'd already left for school, she told Melissa that she needed a break.

She said she needed some time to herself without me, without Melissa and most of all, without Paul. She asked Melissa to look after me and said she'd call when she got to where she was going. According to my sister my mother packed a couple of suitcases and left the house without another word. Paul had yet to return to the house.

"You don't think she did something to him do you?" I asked.

"Shay, I couldn't tell you what that woman has done. She is not the same mother we grew up with." Melissa answered.

"So, now what? I'm not staying here with that man if he happens to show up."

"I know that Aeysha and neither am I. I've been on the phone all morning trying to find somebody we could stay with until Tyrone and I could figure this all out." Melissa shouted.

There was no way to reach Dad, so I guess Melissa and I were truly in a mess. Tyrone's place was simply too small to add three extra people into the mix. Besides that, they had a newborn. My mom's sister said that she couldn't have us at her place because she lived in public housing and could get evicted. Melissa called my grandmother's sister who lived on the other side of downtown. Aunt Vickie said that we could stay with her until we found a more permanent solution.

"So, we have to stay with Aunt Vickie?" I asked disguised by this whole situation.

"For a little while, Aeysha." Lissa said. She was definitely stressed because she never calls me by given name and so far she's done it twice in a matter of minutes. "Ty and Stan are on the way over to help us get our things over to Aunt Vickie's. So, I suggest you start packing and just take the important things."

Still in my uniform, I went down to the garage to get our suitcases. Melissa had begun to take things out of the drawers when I found my way back to the room. I was in a daze. How could Mom just leave us like that? Why would she leave us here, the one place she knew we hated?

Melissa and I packed in silence. I guess there was really nothing to say. Not only was she the mother of a young child, Melissa now had to take care of me. I couldn't even begin to understand what she must have been thinking.

Stan was the first to arrive. I went downstairs to let him in. I was truly happy to see him. I had no idea what Paul would do if he returned home to find Melissa and I here. Stan walked into our room and wrapped his arms around Melissa. That was all it took for her to break down again. He sat with Lissa on the bed until she calmed herself. We'd packed three suitcases by the time Tyrone arrived. He brought along some boxes to make sure we could get everything we wanted to take.

"Sis, don't worry about nothing. We're going to take care of you," he said to me.

"Ty, I just want to get out of here before Paul gets back." I said dryly.

With the four of us at work packing we were done in less than an hour and a half. Melissa went into Paul and Mom's room to get our birth certificates, social security cards and other important papers Mom kept tucked away in a folder in her bottom drawer. Personally, I was surprised it was still there and that Paul hadn't found a way to keep it from us. As Stan and Tyrone carried boxes and suitcases to their cars Paul pulled into the driveway.

"I hope you didn't take anything that didn't belong to you." He said as he approached the front door.

"Unless you want me to finish what I was about to do to you the last time I suggest you back up off my sisters." Tyrone said as he walked up to Paul's face with Stan right behind him.

I silently prayed that Paul wouldn't respond. Lord knows I didn't need my brother going back to jail right then. Paul brushed past us and went into the house.

"Did you guys get everything you wanted?" Ty asked. Melissa and I both nodded. "Well, go wait in the car because if he says one more thing to you, I'm gone bust him up."

We both got into Tyrone's car without saying a word. I strapped Sage into the car seat and then watched out the window as Ty and Stan brought the last of our things out of the house. They put the last of our things in Stan's car, closed the trunks and off we went. Ty pulled away from the house so fast his tires spun hard, burning rubber into the ground.

Our ride to Aunt Vickie's was a very silent one. What could be said? Our mother has just abandoned us like we were nothing. It was all about what she needed. She didn't even stay around long enough to make sure we were safe somewhere away from Paul. She just left us to fend for ourselves. What kind of mother would do that to her children?

"Don't worry, you guys. Everything is going to be fine."

Tyrone's famous last words.

Aunt Vickie was standing in the doorway as we pulled into her driveway. Melissa and I both looked miserable, Melissa more than me because I refused to cry. Mom left no forwarding address, no telephone number and simply no way to reach her at all. I guess she didn't think about the fact that one of us might have an emergency or need blood after a terrible accident. Mom just was not thinking.

How are Melissa, Sage and I supposed to live? What are we supposed to do about money and food? There was no way Melissa could work enough to support me and Sage. Besides, I don't want to be the reason my sister doesn't finish school. She had her heart set on graduation from college and moving on with her life. Having me added to her list of problems just isn't fair. I know my brother will do all he can to help, but he has a family of his own to worry about.

Well, I guess there is really no need to wrack my brain trying to figure out how this whole mess is going to work out. Maybe Mom will come back soon. Maybe all she needed was a week or two to get her thoughts in order. She can't honestly leave us for too long. We're her kids and we need her. I'm sure she knows that.

The Final Chapter

My junior year at ICA was pretty rough. It only took Melissa and me about a month of staying at Aunt Vickie's to know that we were not going to be able to stay there long. She had a small three-bedroom house and two growing boys to feed. Getting up in the mornings was a nightmare. There was only one bathroom and with all of us apparently needing to get out of the house at the same time, Melissa and I just went in the bathroom together.

It was taking me about thirty to forty minutes to get to school on the bus since Aunt Vickie's house was a little further out than our old place. One good thing I can say about my mother is that she had paid a full year of tuition at ICA so Melissa and I decided that I would stay there and at least finish the year. If Mom did decide to come back during the school year, we didn't want to have to explain why I wasn't at ICA. Don't get me wrong, Jo and I thought long and hard about this being our opportunity to kick off our years in high school right, however, in the end Melissa's logic outweighed our plans.

Stan and Tyrone convinced Melissa to start school. She wanted to wait a year to see what was going to happen with Mom and to make sure she could look out for me and Sage. In this instance, Ty and Stan's logic outweighed Melissa's plan. Although she started a couple of weeks late, I'm so very glad they talked her into it. Melissa loved going to school. That was all she talked about every night before we went to bed. She and I spent many Saturdays together at the library studying. I helped her write papers and she helped me with my math.

Just before Thanksgiving Stan had come up with an idea that would change our lives for ever. One Saturday afternoon he picked us up and took us over to Tyrone's because he said he had some great news. I had no clue what he was up to and neither did Melissa. After he got us all to sit down and shut up, he told us that he'd spoken to one of his professors about Melissa and me. Not giving too much detail he explained that we were basically looking for a place to live.

Well it just so happened that this teacher owned an apartment complex and would have a vacant apartment, there was one catch. The apartment complex was in Berkeley. This would make commuting for both me and Melissa a challenge. However, the better news was that she was going to wave the first and last month's rent to help us out. Also, we'd be closer to Tyrone and he could check on us when ever he wanted.

I don't know if I liked the fact that my brother could just pop over when ever he liked but having my own room would definitely be a good thing. The professor's daughter was currently living in the only apartment she had coming vacant by the end of the month. So, we were in.

We spent most of that day weighing the pros and cons of Melissa and I having our own apartment. Melissa was due to start a work study job on campus so that money will help, and we also had the money coming in that Dad sent both of us each month, so we were off to a good start. Thinking about Sage, we knew that he would attend the campus child care and therefore, we wouldn't have the added stress of trying to drop him off or pick him up at a different location.

Tyrone's major concern was that we'd be traveling back and forth across the bridge to school. But that concern was easily reduced when we realized it would have been a little difficult to transfer me to a different school without a parent or guardian's consent. The California Child Protection Agency would have been all over us and more than likely they would have taken me from my brother and sister.

If we were going to do this, we all had to be on the same page and in agreement. Bobbie and Stan thought it was a good idea. Melissa was nervous and Tyrone was still undecided. I just wanted my own room. I really didn't care how I got it, I just wanted it. By the time we'd all gone out to eat and come back, Tyrone finally agreed to let us have the apartment on one condition; Melissa and I had to stay in school no matter what. I could work a part time job after school if I wanted "but no more that twelve hours a week" my brother said.

Stan and Tyrone said they'd both help out as much as they could. Stan helping us with rides a couple of days a week so that we could save on transportation costs and Tyrone helping cover food or a utility bill. Getting a part time job was the least I could do since my brother, sister and Stan were doing everything they could to keep us together.

The End

The sun has shone and set on that part of our lives. Today is my graduation day. I am so very, very excited. My whole family is here with the exception of my father. Apparently, he couldn't take the time off work. After spending about two and a half years on hiatus Mom returned. She moved in with some friends and left Melissa and I to continue life as we'd known it, uninterrupted which was more than fine with us. She sat in the back of the auditorium with her new beau.

The past couple of years had been tough, but we'd made it. My brother and sister made it their business to see that I stood on this stage, in this robe, at this ceremony to receive my diploma. Words could not express how I felt at this moment. Great things seemed to just be flowing our way.

Ty and Bobbie were in the process of buying a new home. Stan had proposed to Melissa on Valentine's Day and the wedding was scheduled for the end of July, so that I could do my bridesmaid thing before shipping out to college in Georgia. Jo and I decided that since we couldn't spend our high school years together, we'd make it up in college. Both of us were accepted to Brown-Atlanta University and could not wait to go. Life has a funny way of working things out after all.

(Author's photo by Beth Grant Photography)

About the Author

Rosetta Mandisa is an educator, blogger and avid reader. Born in San Francisco, California, she had the privilege of spending summers in Alabama with her grandmother where she learned much about her family history. This time with her grandmother sparked a love for African American history.

Graduating from Immaculate Conception Academy in San Francisco, with dreams of working in advertising, she began her higher-level education at San Francisco State University. Later, moving with her son to Florida, it was a negative experience with her son's education and subsequent conversation with her father that changed her career path. Receiving her bachelor's degree in Elementary Education from Nova Southeastern University, she began her teaching career. With a love of learning, she continued her education, receiving a master's degree in Educational Leadership.

She is a strong believer in the saying, "When you know better, you do better." This is what drives her each day to be her very best and to grow through reading, attending motivational seminars and building positive, diverse relationships.

She lives in Florida with her family.